Rally 'Round Green

Other Books by Judy Christie

RALLY 'ROUND GREEN

The Green Series

Judy Christie

Abingdon Press fiction
a novel approach to faith

Nashville, Tennessee

Rally 'Round Green

Copyright © 2011 by Judy Christie

ISBN-13: 978-1-4267-1319-4

Published by Abingdon Press, P.O. Box 801, Nashville, TN 37202

www.abingdonpress.com

The persons and events portrayed in this work of fiction
are the creations of the author, and any resemblance
to persons living or dead is purely coincidental.

Published in association with the Books & Such Literary Agency,
5926 Sunhawk Drive, Santa Rosa, CA 95409,
www.booksandsuch.biz

Cover design by Anderson Design Group, Nashville, TN

Library of Congress Cataloging-in-Publication Data

CIP data [TO COME]

Printed in the United States of America

1 2 3 4 5 6 7 8 9 10 / 16 15 14 13 12 11

*To Kathie Coffey Rowell,
friend, journalist & proud graduate
of Ashland High*

ACKNOWLEDGMENTS

**New Golden Pen Awards Given
from *The Green News-Item*
with heartfelt thanks from Lois Barker Craig—
and Judy Christie**

So many people make going to Green possible, and I thank you all, especially readers who speak so affectionately about what is going on with Lois Barker Craig and crew. A special thanks to the many book clubs who are reading The Green Series.

To those who offer community news items for *The Green News-Item* and provide all sorts of encouragement, I offer another huge thank-you: Alan English, Ginger Hamilton, Karen Enriquez, Lynn Stewart, Virginia Disotell, Craig Durrett, Mary Ann Van Osdell, Martha Fitzgerald, Mary Frances Christie, Pat Lingenfelter, Robin Williams, Kathie Rowell, and Eleanor Ransburg. Thank you, all! Memories of Alisa Stingley, who gave the Green Rabbits their name, are woven through this book.

And my gratitude to Mary Dark, Carol Lovelady, Terrie Roberts, Rita Hummingbird, granddaughter Gracie; agents Etta Wilson and Janet Grant; the fantastic fiction team at Abingdon Press, including Ramona Richards, Julie Dowd, Maegan Roper, Jenny Youngman, and Holly Quick; and, always, to my wonderful husband, Paul.

1

*A sheriff's deputy says Melva Murphy assaulted her
husband, Harry, when he complained about a meal she
cooked. Melva says she thought the pepper spray was
a good response to his request for more seasoning.
Harry chose not to press charges.*

—The Green News-Item

A steady stream of people filed past the stranger, but he never spoke, even when jostled.

Scanning the crowd and occasionally jotting something in a small notepad, he didn't seem to be looking *for* anyone, just looking. He was dressed more for a business meeting than a pep rally and was definitely an odd addition to this Green gathering.

"Lois! Is there room up there for us?"

My friend Kevin interrupted my spying, waving as she yelled. Her toddler son, Asa Corinthian, gave a delighted squeal and ran toward me, pulling his mother up the ten or so wooden rows. The duo wove through friends, neighbors, and Kevin's patients, the boy trying to work loose from his mother's hand and calling my name in his childish voice.

"Do you always have to sit on the top row?" Kevin asked as Asa plopped down in my lap. She was, of course, not breathing hard and had the casual, sophisticated look I couldn't achieve if my life depended on it. She smelled like Dove soap and her dark hair was swept into a French twist.

"These are the best seats in the house," I said, kissing the little boy's head. "I get some of my best story ideas up here."

Kevin rolled her eyes. "Quit acting like you're working. You're admiring that good-looking husband of yours. Look, Asa, there's Coach Chris." She waved at Chris, who was looking handsome as he stood under the basketball goal.

Her son squirmed, giggled, and yelled. My husband probably couldn't hear Asa over the hubbub of Green residents, but a broad smile crossed his face as he gave a thumbs-up sign before turning toward a row of chairs and a handmade lectern.

My eyes went back to the stranger, who stepped out to the edge of the court and watched Chris walk over to a small group of teachers, all wearing Green Rabbits T-shirts. Briefly the man settled on the end of the front row, adjusting his trouser legs, but then stood and brushed off his pants, a frown marring his classic good looks.

Members of the student council and honor society milled around the end of the court, flirting with cheerleaders. A teen from Grace Chapel waved to me and did a series of back flips.

"Don't you think those skirts are a little too short?" I pointed to the pep squad.

"They're adorable," Kevin said. "Much cuter than the uniforms we had when I was in school here."

"You won't think they're quite so cute when Asa gets ready to date." I gave her son, eager to get down to the court, a hug.

"Aren't you rushing things a bit? He's not even in kindergarten yet."

"Time goes fast," I said. "It'll be fun to watch him play for Chris, won't it?"

Kevin smiled and seemed to gaze into the future at Asa as a teenager. With Chris and me already approaching forty, we would be in our fifties by then. *Oh my!*

The high school and middle school bands marched in, cymbals clashing, as we chatted. Honor students, many of whom were in Chris's history classes, passed out agendas, reproduced on the school's ancient photocopier. The elementary school choir lined up at center court, mirroring the big smile their director gave.

"This is one of my favorite events of the year." Kevin studied the program. "I know every one of these children."

"The town's pediatrician usually knows the kids," I said.

"True, but I've known their parents and their grandparents, too. There's something special about the January Rabbit Rally."

"Part musical, part athletic exhibition, part awards ceremony," I said. "What else could you wish for?"

"As far back as I can remember, this has been a tradition in Green," Kevin said. "Look at those darling little children standing near the big kids. It won't be long till those little ones will be the big ones. . . ."

"Now who's rushing things?"

My beautiful friend picked up her son and bounced him on her knee, her voice tender. "Asa, that's one of the many reasons Mommy wants to raise you in Green. We've been doing this since I was in kindergarten. We'll be doing it when your children are in kindergarten."

The boy giggled and reached for Kevin's gold-hoop earring, oblivious to the tears glistening in her eyes.

"You're awfully nostalgic tonight," I said. "Is everything OK?"

"I feel sentimental." She kissed the top of Asa's head. "It finally seems as though things are settling down after the tornado. *Normal* is probably too strong a word, but nights like tonight sure feel good."

I felt the emotion, too.

"With things almost back to normal, I thought you might bring Terrence tonight." I nudged my shoulder against hers.

Kevin shot me a mild mind-your-business look. "You said you were going to quit trying to push us together. He's overloaded with cases and can't drive up to Green all the time."

"You're keeping him at arm's length," I said. Terrence D'Arbonne was a handsome, high-profile lawyer in Alexandria who had helped me with a legal jam at the paper. He adored Kevin and Asa.

In her early thirties, Kevin insisted she had her hands full with her adopted child, the challenges of being the only African-American doctor in town, and staying connected with her parents. I wanted her to fall in love and get married, the way I had.

"They're getting ready to start the ceremony," Kevin said.

"Nice change of subject."

The crowd quieted as the principal walked to the middle of the gym, nearly tripping over the microphone cord, resulting in a loud squealing noise. The children's choir members covered their ears, and one youngster bolted for his mother, never returning for the musical numbers.

Eugene Ellis had been Green's principal since Chris was in school, head of the elementary, middle and high schools, housed on the same campus. In his mid-sixties, he had dressed up for this occasion, wearing a Rabbits golf shirt instead of the regular school T-shirt.

He smiled and greeted the audience like a grandfather saying hello to his grandchildren, firing them up as much as the cheerleaders had.

"I bring greetings from Mayor Eva Hillburn, who is out of town on city business. She sends her congratulations on the excellent school year under way and her best wishes for the semester ahead." The crowd applauded loudly, drowning out the squawking of the public address system. "Green has the hardest-working student body and faculty you will find anywhere."

Teachers and administrators, including the assistant principal who had started after the Christmas break, handed out awards, bringing rambunctious applause. The final honor brought the gym to its feet.

"The award for top scholar-athlete goes to Anthony Cox," Mr. Ellis said. "Anthony, you show courage, leadership, and academic excellence. You epitomize what a Green senior should be."

"Oh," I murmured, watching the tall, muscular young man I knew so well walk forward. Without a father and surviving the abuse of his mother's former boyfriend, Anthony never gave up. "He's such a great guy."

"He's already overcome more than most of us ever will," Kevin said.

Molly, part-time newspaper employee, college student and Anthony's girlfriend, cheered and clapped. My employee Tammy, photographing the event for the *News-Item*, let out one of her ear-piercing whistles.

The unknown man neither smiled nor clapped, making my mind drift from the program.

"Don't look right now, Kevin, but do you know that guy by the door?" I spoke right into her ear, trying to be heard over the noise.

She immediately turned, and I made instant eye contact with the man.

"I said, don't look," I hissed.

"I couldn't help it." She acted as though she hadn't been caught staring. "I don't recall ever seeing him."

"He's taking notes. I wonder if he could be a reporter from out-of-town."

"He's dressed way too nice to be a reporter," Kevin said.

"He could be a television announcer doing a follow-up," I said, ignoring her dig. "With the anniversary of the tornado coming up, we'll probably have another group of journalists in town."

"Maybe he's trying to scoop you," she said. "Isn't that what you hotshot newspaper owners call it?"

I threw her a look similar to the ones she gave me when I meddled about Terrence. "No one scoops *The Green News-Item* on its home turf."

In the commotion of the post-rally reception, Iris Jo, my office manager and former neighbor on Route Two, grabbed my arm.

"Can you serve the punch?" She sounded agitated, rare for her. "The new assistant principal was supposed to, but I can't find her anywhere."

"At your service," I said. "Don't you need to sit down for a while?"

"Lois, I've told you before. I'm a cancer patient, not a former prisoner of war. I feel great, and I'll feel even better when you stand over there and ladle small amounts of ginger ale and lime sherbet into those cute paper cups."

"Yikes!" a voice said behind me. "Iris sounded like me there for a minute." Tammy snapped a picture of us.

"This is my first event as president of the Booster Club, and things are out of sync," Iris said. "I need to go make sure the pep squad hasn't set the popcorn machine on fire. Take care of the punch, please."

Assuming my position at the bowl, I filled dozens of cups, Iris Jo swooping in to add giant plastic bottles of ginger ale. "Try to stretch it," she whispered. "Our club funds are running low, and the turnout's large, as always."

"Should I start charging per cup?" I joked. "Some people have had thirds."

"Kids," she said with a soft laugh.

"I'm talking about the adults."

She walked off, trim and healthy despite her surgery and months of chemotherapy.

"The Booster Club can carry out a theme, can't they?" Tammy asked, handing me a bag of popcorn that had been dyed green.

While I chewed, uncertain about eating green popcorn, she took photos of Anna Grace, the newspaper's food writer, serving the last slices of a green cake. The older woman promised a parent she would include the recipe in next week's column, and visited with a woman who had called to complain about the newspaper's "poor coverage" of garden club activities.

"E-mail me your favorite cake recipes," Anna Grace said. "I've heard your chocolate pound cake never turns out dry." The woman, who had been cranky with me, glowed at the compliment.

"Hi, Mrs. Craig." A deep, affectionate voice spoke right into my ear, sending shivers down my spine.

"Hello, Coach Craig." I leaned up to give Chris a peck on the lips. Although it had only been a few hours since I had talked to him, I felt my heart speed up—I was still amazed he was my husband. "Could I interest you in a cup of green punch?"

"I couldn't believe my eyes when I saw you serving punch," he said, gulping the drink. "I thought you had to leave early to write editorials."

"Apparently the new assistant principal is AWOL, and I can't say 'no' to Iris Jo," I said and dabbed at melted sherbet on Chris's upper lip.

Wearing sherbet or not, he looked every bit the experienced coach as he turned to visit with a parent. A line of people interrupted our chat, slapping him on the back and saying how much they were enjoying basketball season.

I wasn't the only one in Green who loved Chris Craig.

"I suppose I'd better circulate," he said. "Am I permitted to kiss the kitchen help again?"

"Most definitely." I leaned in for a brief embrace.

A sound like a pack of howling dogs erupted, and I looked over to see most of the basketball team cheering us on with an annoying chant.

"Don't pay any attention to them, Lois," Molly said, walking up hand-in-hand with Anthony.

"They're immature," the basketball player said with a grin and hung his head shyly when we congratulated him on his honor.

"Do I still get to write the story on the rally?" Molly asked. Wearing one of Anthony's many jerseys, she held up a reporter's notebook. "Katy is going to be so jealous."

"That's what she gets for going away to school. If you have time, the story's yours," I said. "Be sure to get quotes from Mr. Ellis."

"That man is a great principal," Chris said. "This school means as much to him now as it did when I started teaching nearly twenty years ago."

As the teens wandered off, Chris checked his watch with a slight frown. "I've got to run to a faculty meeting," he said.

"Tonight?" I asked. "After teaching all day?"

"The new assistant principal has set up committees for something, and Eugene says we need to pay attention to her." Chris glanced around to make sure no one was listening. "She's a hot-shot education expert sent in by the state. I think he's a little put off by her."

"Maybe it should be the other way around," I said. "I hope you don't have to stay too late." I reached up to give him another quick kiss.

"Is that appropriate?" A terse female voice caused me to jump back from Chris, surprised that someone stood so near. It was the new administrator, a displeased look on her not-a-day-over-thirty face. In slacks and a blazer, she carried an air of authority, her long hair pulled back with a silver barrette and a stern slant to her mouth.

"Newlyweds," I said, forcing a laugh and holding out my hand. "I'm Lois Barker Craig, Chris's wife. I apologize that I haven't gotten by to meet you."

She gave my hand a quick shake. "Priscilla Robinson, curriculum specialist for Green." Her clipped tone was colder than the sherbet in the punch I had been ladling. "Coach Craig, it does not set a good example for you to display affection at a school gathering."

"You're kidding, right?" I asked before Chris could respond.

"Lois . . ." Chris said in the soft warning tone he used when he thought I was about to say something he would regret.

"It's time for the meeting, if you can pull yourself away, Coach," the woman said.

The look on Chris's face was one usually reserved for disrespectful players on other teams and the occasional hostile coach. Clearly not intimidated by the new administrator, he hugged me. "I'll see you at the house. Be careful driving home."

The woman practically growled as she set off to corral other faculty members, including Mr. Ellis, who laughed and talked with a group of parents until she snared him. He looked dismayed but turned to follow Priscilla Robinson like she was the Pied Piper.

Chris looked back at me, smiled, and winked. I grimaced, perturbed by the woman's manner.

"She's a piece of work, isn't she?" Tammy asked, following my eyes. "She's got an ego bigger that Bouef Parish."

Sipping a cup of punch and fuming, I agreed and surveyed the room. Anna Grace and her brand-new husband, Bud, the agriculture columnist, were cleaning up cake crumbs. Iris Jo and Stan, a newspaper couple who had wed only days after last year's tornado, picked up stray programs and other trash. Molly and Anthony emptied big plastic garbage cans.

As usual, everyone pitched in, and Priscilla Robinson was as out of place as a tropical fish in one of my husband's catfish ponds.

A movement from the kitchen caught my eye, and I turned to see the stranger opening oven doors, examining the seal on the refrigerator, even trying the sprayer on the commercial dishwasher.

I watched until I couldn't stand it any longer and walked toward the serving line, where many of the students got free breakfasts and lunches each day.

"May I help you find something?" I asked.

"I've already found what I was looking for," he said and walked past me and into the foyer, near the office.

Curious and uneasy, I followed a few steps behind him as he slipped through the front doors and into the night.

⁕

Tammy was arguing in the lobby. Her voice had the not-quite-but-almost rude tone she used when she was pushed.

"As I have said three times, we are not set up for delivery to motel rooms. However, we do have newspaper racks around town."

Holly Beth, my one-year-old Yorkie, growled from the chair where she slept, apparently annoyed at having her nap interrupted by newspaper business. Perhaps I should have left her in the kitchen at home, but I had gotten used to her coming to work with me.

I got up from my desk and walked closer to the door, wondering if I should intervene. Tammy was a little . . . high-strung . . . but she was usually good with customers. I stood back and strained to hear. Tammy's voice carried, but the man's voice was soft.

"I'm willing to pay extra if necessary, honey," he said.

"I am not your honey, and we cannot guarantee next-day delivery on mail subscriptions, even if you pay extra. I don't care how they do it in Houston or Dallas, or wherever you said you're from."

"I'm from Austin," the man said, his tone more clipped now. "The state capital."

"The capital of Louisiana is Baton Rouge," Tammy said. "I don't pay much attention to what goes on over in Texas."

"Perhaps you should," the man said.

Holly Beth sat up and gave a sharp bark. It was definitely time for me to step in.

I pasted on my biggest newspaper-owner smile as I walked into the lobby. "Good morning, sir," I said. "Is there something . . ."

I stopped mid-sentence, face-to-face with the mystery man from the school pep rally the night before. He looked as though he'd never seen me before, and I plunged ahead. "Is there something I can help you with?"

"I certainly hope so," he said.

"I was handling this," Tammy muttered at the same time. "He wants to get two subscriptions to the *Item*."

"We can always use more subscribers," I said.

"We most certainly can," Tammy said. "But we cannot control the U.S. Postal Service, and we cannot guarantee next-day delivery without exorbitant charges."

"I apologize if I gave you the wrong impression," the man said, his eyes surveying the receptionist's figure a moment longer than appropriate. "I'm happy to pay the fee."

"Excellent," I said. "We'll invoice you." I shot her my publisher look and turned back to the man. "Are you relocating to Green?"

Before he could answer, Holly Beth ran under the swinging gate to the front door. She barked wildly as Mayor Eva and Sugar Marie entered.

"Look, Sugar, it's your sweet puppy." The mayor's voice shifted to baby talk when the dogs were involved. "How's our darling girl today?"

The man got very still, similar to his stance at the pep rally. After what seemed like minutes, although it had only been a moment or two, Eva looked up with a smile, which quickly disappeared.

"Marc?" she asked. Her voice sounded hoarse.

"Hello, Eva." He greeted her with a husky warmth to his voice and an almost flirtatious smile. "You haven't changed a bit."

"What brings you to Green?" Eva did not sound at all like her usual in-charge self. Tammy and I exchanged a quick glance.

"Business," he said, reaching out to put his hand on her shoulder. "I hear you're the mayor. Congratulations."

Eva jerked as though she had brushed up against a hot iron, and both Holly Beth and Sugar Marie snarled. Having been bitten by Sugar Marie, I wanted to warn him to be careful about touching the mayor.

Bumping into the door as she backed up, Eva firmed her mouth into a straight line and narrowed her eyes. She bent over and petted Holly Beth, then scooped up Sugar Marie. "Lois, I'll call you later."

"I'll walk out with you," the man she had called Marc said, and fell in behind her before she could speak.

"But we didn't get your subscription straight," Tammy said. The door swung shut on her words.

2

*Next month's Groundhog Day community dinner will
be a catered event after last year's food-poisoning scare.
"There wasn't any food poisoning at all—just a prank
by drama students at the high school," said Virginia
Knox. "Still, we thought we'd better be safe than sorry.
Besides, Hank's Bayou Catfish puts on a great spread
with all the fixin's. Hope you'll come out for a delicious
meal and to see if we're in for more winter."*

—The Green News-Item

Every time I pulled into the driveway at home my heart soared. Right before it plummeted.

I wondered if everyone in the midst of a remodeling project felt like this.

The stately old house looked as though it had sat on this spot for decades—except for the scar where it was spliced together and the equipment where there used to be grass and the general look of a bomb having exploded.

It was gorgeous . . . and stressful.

Chris arrived home right behind me, pulling his muddy pickup in next to my muddy car, his headlights sweeping across the mess, shining for a moment on the stained glass in the carved front door propped against the boarded-up opening. Holly Beth went crazy, yapping and whining. Me, she liked. But she adored my husband and the three dogs he brought to our marriage.

When I opened the car door, I tried to hold on to her, knowing she'd be muddy in moments. Everything around our home on Route Two was muddy. I stepped in it. Got it on my clothes.

"Do you ever feel like you've got mud in your mouth?" I asked as I stepped out to greet Chris.

"Maybe I'll pass on that kiss I was about to give you." He walked toward me with a grin, illuminated by the light from a temporary post at the edge of the house. "Most wives greet their husbands with something like, 'Hi, honey, how was your day?'"

He embraced me and tried to work in a kiss without dropping the squirming Holly Beth.

"I'm amazed at how much mud there is," I said, loving his solid feel. "I find it in the strangest places. I took my calendar out of my purse at work today, and there was mud on it. I pulled my hair into a ponytail, and I had mud on my neck. Where does it come from?"

"Now that's a question I can answer. Behold." Chris swung his arm around as though giving a tour. "Our yard."

On this early January evening, the disarray was apparent even in the winter gloom. The tornado nearly a year ago had ripped out a few gorgeous old trees, and the steady convoy of work vehicles left ruts that got deeper by the day. Damage remained from the two gargantuan trucks that had moved the pieces of the old house onto the land three months earlier. I shivered and pulled my coat closer, Louisiana dampness seeping in.

"Is it worth it?" Chris asked, taking the little dog from me and patting her. "Should we have moved into town?"

"Wait a minute," I said, poking him in the chest. "My husband never second-guesses himself. That's my job."

He laughed, put Holly Beth down, and drew me closer. "You haven't answered my question."

"It's worth it." I looked past the mess to the beauty of the structure. My eyes went to the front door again, a work of art in need of a facelift. "Although you may have to remind me of that every now and then."

We walked toward the back of the house, where Mannix, Markey, and Kramer barked and ran up and down behind the fence that attempted to keep them in. Within minutes they'd be out in the mud, Mannix, with only three legs, leading the way by climbing over the gate.

"So how was your day?" I asked, stooping to pet each of the animals and trying to avoid their dirty paws.

"The usual," he said. "The bureaucracy gets harder and harder to deal with, and students need more help."

He walked up the makeshift side steps and opened the back door, the only functional entry into the house. "No point in standing out in the cold talking about it."

The dogs scooted past us into the improvised laundry room, and I handed each of them a treat from a box on the washing machine.

"This is one of my favorite parts of the day," I said as Chris took off his coat.

"That's a great thing about these mutts." He patted each one again. "They're always happy to see us. They don't care about test scores."

"Or testy administrators," I added.

We began the ritual of pouring food for each, replenishing their water and talking nonsense to them.

"When I hand them a dog biscuit, the outside world evaporates," I said. "It's like a benediction on the day." Chris looked at me with an odd expression, and I felt self-conscious. "Does that sound too corny?"

"It sounds like one of the many reasons I married you," he said. "And you say you're not a dog person."

"I'm not!" I pulled the gate across the open door into the kitchen, Holly Beth impatiently following us to her dish next to the refrigerator. "Or not much anyway."

We both laughed.

"Tammy's always telling me I've gone to the dogs. She thinks that's hilarious."

"It is pretty funny," Chris said.

"She says I wasn't barking up the wrong tree when I started dating you."

My husband groaned. "I surrender. No more Tammy puns. Let's have supper and enjoy being home at a decent hour."

"Don't tell anybody, but I skipped the Friends of the Library meeting tonight. I never did that before I got married."

"I didn't even get my grades entered after basketball practice. We have meeting after meeting after meeting these days."

"It's too much." I moved around the cramped kitchen. "We're camping out in three rooms at home, and work is so . . . constant."

"At least we aren't in the travel trailer. I don't step on Holly Beth every time I turn around or bump my shin on that antique table Rose gave you."

I pulled out a frozen casserole, part of a steady stream of food from my mother-in-law. Although my cooking had improved over the past year, I still was no match for Estelle Craig.

"You shower, and I'll finish getting dinner ready," I said.

"I've already had dinner."

"You ate?"

"This is supper." He grinned and headed into the bedroom, also currently the living room and computer area. "I had dinner at noon in the school cafeteria. What are you? A Yankee or something?"

"Civilized people call that lunch," I yelled after him. "And you are not a Yankee if you're from Ohio. That's the Midwest. Hurry up or you're going to miss dinner."

I hummed as I dug around in the big plastic box that served as a cabinet, not sure if the pan I was looking for was in the travel trailer or had blown away. Finding what I needed, I looked at the three big dogs, who turned around in circles and lay down on their muddy rugs with contented sighs.

I knew the feeling.

───⚬☙⚬───

The dogs barked when headlights pulled into the driveway.

Chris, reaching for his second helping of corn casserole, groaned and rolled his eyes. "I guess it's too much to hope that someone's turning around."

I sighed.

A light knock sounded on the side door and Chris pushed his chair back, running his fingers through his still-damp hair, always a tad long.

Before he went further, Holly Beth ran around the table and to the back door, her high-pitched yelp a dead giveaway.

"Mayor Eva," Chris and I said at the same time.

With the door scarcely open, Sugar Marie jumped out of Eva's arms and began to roll around with Holly Beth, growling and barking. The other three dogs joined in, jumping and running, one of them producing a grubby rubber ball covered in drool.

"Ahh, quiet country living," I said. "Welcome, Eva. I hope you brought your ear plugs."

"I'm sorry to interrupt, but I didn't think this could wait." The mayor, still dressed in the wool suit she had worn at the newspaper office earlier, slipped out of her coat, her clothes unwrinkled and spotless, as though the day were getting started instead of wrapping up.

I glanced down at my white overalls, a large rip where I had caught the knee on a nail, and the long-sleeve Florida shirt Pastor Jean loaned me when my clothes blew away. I had never gotten around to giving it back, and it came in handy in the drafty old house.

"Join us for a bite to eat," Chris said, already rummaging for a plate from a half-stocked cupboard. "Lois whipped up a good supper."

"With the help of my mother-in-law."

"I didn't come to eat." Eva protested, and for a moment she looked worn out. "I need to talk to Lois."

"Talk while you eat," Chris said. "There's enough here to feed an army."

Reluctantly Eva put her coat into my hands, and I wondered if she noticed the mud on my shirt and the floor. The white carpet at her house never had a smudge on it. I hoped her coat would be so lucky.

"How are the renovations?" she asked, arranging her silverware in precise order.

"Slow," I said.

"Great," Chris said.

We all laughed.

"I'm not the most patient person, as you may have noticed," I said. "I have a new favorite accessory . . . a tool belt."

"Lois is great with a paintbrush and hammer," my husband said, sounding both proud and surprised. "But I miscalculated what a job this would be."

"Moving a house and putting it back together is similar to building a new house," Eva said. "Except you get to live inside while you're at it. That can't be easy."

"It makes your brother's travel trailer seem almost luxurious," I said.

"Keep it as long as you want. As he said, and I quote, 'It doesn't do me no good while I'm in the hoosegow.'" Eva's smile was strained. Major Wilson, local Realtor, politician, car dealer, and brother of the mayor, was serving time for a long list of crimes, some of which had affected me in one way or another. I knew it hurt Eva that he had done so much harm to the town of Green.

"We've got tools stored in it now," Chris said, "and one of the workers may move in for a while."

The mayor finally started eating, briefly closing her eyes.

"Everything all right?" I asked.

"It's been a long day. It feels good to sit here in your comfortable kitchen."

Chris and I exchanged what I thought of as our married look, the one where we understood what the other was thinking. "If it's OK with you two, I'll take the dogs for a short walk," he said. "Maybe they'll give me some of their energy."

He walked to the row of hooks near the washing machine and lifted his jacket, sending the dogs into a new frenzy. Sugar Marie ran back over to the Mayor and gave a quick bark before heading out.

The house had a glorious moment of quiet as Chris pulled the door shut. I heard him call each of the animals by name and knew he was smiling.

Eva nibbled on a piece of French bread and, if it was possible, sat up straighter in the chair. In her late fifties, she was an attractive woman, warm but not effusive. The few streaks of gray in her brown hair had appeared in the weeks after the tornado.

"I know you and Chris don't get much time alone together," she said. "I apologize again for arriving at dinnertime."

"We're always happy to have you." I didn't rush her, still trying to break my habit of prodding people before they were ready to speak.

"I thought you might be interested in that encounter at the paper today."

"Interested? I'm about to die of curiosity, and you know it. Why did you rush off when you saw that man? I haven't seen you move that fast since those out-of-town journalists hounded you."

"I'd rather spend a month with those journalists than deal with Marc." The mayor looked at me as though trying to decide how much to say, and I couldn't stand the silence.

"I saw him at the Rabbit Rally and then he shows up at the *News-Item*, getting Tammy all riled up," I said. "She's not the calmest person, but she usually doesn't get in a fight with people who want to buy a copy of the paper. Is this something bad?"

"I'm not sure."

"But you're sure about everything, Eva."

"Not this. Marc is a consultant, one of those high-priced experts who travel around the country to tell people what they're doing wrong. He wouldn't divulge who he's working for in Green. Without a doubt, he'd like to see me grovel."

She poked at the food on her plate.

"I've spent the last few hours trying to figure out what brought this particular consultant to this specific town, and I haven't gotten anywhere."

"You obviously don't like him." I could hear Chris and the dogs in the driveway. I hoped to get to the bottom of this before they burst back in. "How do you know him?"

"He was a doctoral student when I was an undergraduate, all those years ago." She almost seemed to look back into the past. "I fell in love with him, but he ran off with the student secretary in the College of Education. He seems to have a talent for wooing beautiful young women."

"You must have had quite a thing for him. That's been years ago."

"When he took up with another woman," Eva said, "Marc Hillburn and I had just celebrated our first wedding anniversary."

3

*Fran Phillips of Ringgold lodged a complaint against
her minister after the church bulletin said Fran needed
prayer following cosmetic surgery. "That was plain
gossip," Fran said. "My nips, tucks and what-nots
are no one's business."*

—*The Green News-Item*

Molly closed the door of her mammoth car as though it
were a priceless collectible, but that didn't seem to work. She
opened it again and slammed it with all her might and wiped
her hands as though finishing off a major chore.

Iris and I, headed back from lunch at the Cotton Boll Café,
turned to each other and smiled. The car was a dozen years
old, with enough miles on it to have circumnavigated the
globe a few times. Formerly owned by a soap salesman, it had
the odor of detergent and a trunk larger than most late-model
cars.

Molly couldn't have been prouder. She had gotten her
driver's license only weeks before the purchase, running over
a duck and squirrel while taking the test. "The driving guy
agreed that neither of the accidents was my fault," she said,
flashing her new license. "But I was so shaken up that my picture turned out horrible."

Today she wrestled with the back door, pulled out her back-pack, and once more threw her weight into closing the piece of heavy metal. She tenderly tapped the roof of the car, said something we couldn't hear, and headed in to the newspaper.

"Do you think she's named it yet?" Iris asked.

"Probably first, middle, and last names."

Iris moved at a steady pace as we passed the newspaper office and started on our daily loop around downtown. "It's the first car anyone in her family has ever owned. Her mother has either walked to work or caught a ride to the nursing home for years."

Iris walked with purpose, committed to daily exercise in a way I had never managed. Her hair had grown back, covering her head in a short brown cap. Her skin glowed, and I wasn't sure if that was due to her improved health or her marriage to Stan. I panted to keep up, nearly sweating on the chilly winter day. "You're wearing me out. Do you think Molly would come pick me up in that land yacht of hers?"

Iris cut her eyes at me, and I grumbled but kept walking. "How in the world is she going to afford gas to drive to Alexandria three times a week?" I asked. Maybe if I could draw Iris into conversation, she'd be out of breath, too.

"She'll earn it, same way she bought that car. She's the hardest working young woman I've ever seen."

"I wish she had let us help her buy something a little . . . smaller? Or cuter?"

"You know good and well Molly wanted to do this on her own. She's working her way through that list of hers." A few weeks earlier she had shared her "life list" with us, an idea she and Katy had come up with. Each of the young women was working on her dreams, which included going to Europe together one day and making lots of money.

"She's checking off a lot of things," I said. "She graduated from high school, enrolled in college, bought a car, works full time at the *Item*."

"From that smile on Molly's face," Iris said, "I'd say she's finally got a few things going right in her life."

"When I was her age, I didn't have a car *or* a boyfriend."

"With Katy at school, Molly and Anthony spend a lot of time together." Iris turned toward Bayou Lake. "I was so pleased he was honored the other night."

"Chris says he's one of the best all-around players he's ever coached."

"He's fun to watch," Iris Jo said. "I just hope that private school in Shreveport doesn't recruit him."

"They'd better not!" I exclaimed. "They stole two of our best guys after the storm."

As the wife of the Green High coach, I had gotten used to talking about sports, anytime, anywhere. Iris Jo and Stan attended every game, no matter the sport. Like most people in Green, they enjoyed watching and discussing teams, especially their beloved Rabbits. The entire town turned out for football, basketball, and baseball, putting aside differences of any type to cheer on the school.

Walking back into the newspaper, we nearly bumped into Molly, who was dashing down the steps. "I'm sorry, Lois, but I've got to leave for a few minutes. My sister's sick, and I need to pick her up at school. I won't be long. Mama will be off work soon."

"No rush," Iris said before I could. "We're caught up on filing, and I can help Tammy with calendar listings."

"Sebastian and I will be right back." She yanked hard on the driver's door on her car.

"Sebastian?" I asked.

"My new car," she said with a grin. "Isn't he cute?" With a wave, she drove off.

Within an hour she was back in the *Item's* composing room, working on the second section for the next day's paper. As I came out of the business office, she threw down a blue highlighter.

"Do you need a hand, Molly?" Tammy asked, half-turning from a computer to watch Molly. Holly Beth was asleep on her newsroom bed, a big pillow the staff had given her for Christmas.

"You already did the calendar for me," the girl said. "I can pull my weight around here."

"Never said you couldn't," Tammy said in a gentler tone than she ever used with me. "Everybody needs a hand now and then."

Tempted to jump in, I wondered where their conversation was going. I wasn't eavesdropping, but I didn't want to interrupt. Or that's what I told myself.

"You went to Green High, right?" Molly asked Tammy.

A look of something akin to apprehension passed over the photographer's face. "Of course," she said, suddenly concentrating on the computer screen.

"And Green Elementary and Green Middle School?"

"Sure, same as you," Tammy said. "That's the way it generally works when you grow up in Green."

"Green schools are good schools, right?"

"Seem to be." Tammy stopped what she was doing, stood up, and stretched, looking like a college student herself in navy slacks and slinky T-shirt with a thin sweater. She wandered up to look over Molly's shoulder, as though inspecting the page. "You having trouble with college?"

"I'm making all As," the younger girl said, almost sounding offended. "But while I was waiting in the office to check my sister out, I overheard that new assistant principal. She was telling someone on the phone what a crummy school Green has."

"I met her at the Rabbit Rally," Tammy said. "She's one of those cranky know-it-alls like Lois used to be."

Molly gasped.

"Lois, I know you're listening at the door," Tammy said. "You might as well join the conversation."

I eased into the room, stopping to pet Holly Beth as though I had been headed that way all along.

"Tammy doesn't really think you were a cranky know-it-all when you moved here," Molly said.

"Yes I do." The photographer/receptionist/clerk shot me a teasing look and fiddled with one of the dozens of inexpensive, chunky necklaces she owned, this one bright blue. "But at least Lois was a nice know-it-all. That new woman at the school is plain mean."

With my own history, I felt obligated to defend the administrator, even though she had instantly rubbed me the wrong way. "It takes time to settle into Green," I said. "She'll find out what a good school we have."

"I hope so," Molly said. "She snapped at me when my sister came into the office, and I told her Monique wasn't sick when she left for school. That woman shooed us out of the office. She said she had more important things to do than stand around and argue with me."

"Chris says schools are under a lot of pressure from the state, with new rules every day," I said. "She's probably overwhelmed."

"Overwhelming is more like it," Tammy said.

"Maybe it's time I paid her an official 'welcome to Green' call," I said.

"Maybe you can figure out what she's doing here," Molly said. "She doesn't seem to fit in very well."

"You're not going to get Chris in trouble, are you?" Tammy asked. "She is his boss."

"The coach reports to the principal. Besides, Chris has been a teacher and coach forever. He has more clout in this town than I do. I can't get him in trouble."

"I know what Walt would tell me," Tammy said. She loved to quote her attorney husband, whom she had married on a beach in Florida less than six months ago. "He'd say to keep my nose out of other people's business."

"And would you?"

"Probably not," Tammy said. "But Walt wouldn't be happy about it, and I doubt Chris will either."

"I'm a journalist and a business owner," I said. "This is what I do. Chris knows that."

"One thing's for sure," Tammy said. "If they're up to something at the school, we'll be the first to know."

———※———

A student worker ushered me into Priscilla Robinson's cramped office nearly a week later, the first time the assistant principal could work me into her schedule. I was annoyed at being put off, and the fact that she was nowhere to be seen irritated me further.

At first I sat in the fake leather chair across from her desk, but felt like a recalcitrant student, so I roamed around the room, noticing Ivy League diplomas for bachelor's and master's programs and a host of framed awards, including a teacher-of-the-year honor from a school district in West Texas.

I refrained, but only barely, from looking at the paperwork on her desk, and pulled a book from an old shelf that sat under the long windows. The fluorescent light buzzed and flickered, giving me a headache, and the old radiator clattered and emitted a smell similar to the one at the cleaners where I dropped off my nicest clothes.

Someone tapped on the door, and I put the book back in place and turned with a broad smile. My husband, not Priscilla, stood in the door, every bit the good-looking teacher in his long-sleeved plaid shirt and khakis.

"Lois? What are you doing here?"

"I have a business meeting with the new administrator."

"What are you up to?" he asked, a look in his eyes that said he knew me too well to believe I was here to chitchat.

"I promise I'm not here to stir things up."

"I beg your pardon," an icy voice said. "Is this my office or is it some sort of community gathering spot?"

I felt my face get warm, but Chris turned slowly, his usual patient self. "I came to talk to you about the new computer grading system," he said. "I didn't realize you and Lois had a meeting."

"It seems as though *The Green News-Item* has a keen interest in our local schools, Coach Craig," Priscilla said. "Perhaps you could give me pointers on buttering her up."

"You're on your own there, ma'am," Chris said. "The newspaper's been good to our schools, so maybe it won't be too hard."

He smiled at me and nodded at the woman, who I knew suddenly was his boss, despite my earlier argument otherwise. "I'll get back with you later about the grading compliance questions. See you tonight, Lois."

"Pull the door shut behind you," Miss Robinson said, and Chris nodded. I heard him chatting with the student at the office counter, and the old-fashioned bells jingled on the main office door as he left.

"Have a seat," Priscilla said, and for the briefest moment I couldn't remember why I had set up this meeting. I wished Chris and I were home together on Route Two, working on one of our house projects instead of in what felt like enemy territory.

I took an uncomfortable chair near the window, liking the way the mid-afternoon light highlighted the bare trees in the school yard. I could hear children giggling at recess.

Instead of sitting, Priscilla leaned against the desk, toned legs crossed at the ankles, arms folded across her chest. Her knee-length skirt and matching jacket were dressy for a Green meeting, especially something at the school, and her high heels looked uncomfortable for trotting around campus. I couldn't keep from hoping her feet hurt.

Her stance left no doubt she was accustomed to being a power player, and she had the wardrobe to prove it—even if her office was small and stifling. I had dealt with scores of her type in my days as city editor in Dayton, from executive-wannabes to big-city politicians to corporate colleagues.

She was a mid-level manager at the school, a transplant whose job appeared to be filling out reports and inflicting statistics on hard-working teachers. I wanted to think I was a bigger person than to let her get under my skin.

"Has your move to Green gone smoothly?" I asked.

"Not particularly," she said. "But I'm sure you didn't ask for this meeting to talk about my fight with a trucking company, nor my landlord's apparent inability to get my heat working." The radiator made a knocking noise at that moment, and she looked at it with scorn. Almost satisfied scorn, if there were such a thing. "What can I do for you, Ms. Craig?"

"Lois," I said. "Call me Lois. That whole Ms. Craig thing makes me feel like my mother-in-law."

"Well, Lois, let's get this interview going." She glanced at her watch, her impatience reminding me of my early days in Green.

I hoped she'd catch on to the Green pace soon, for all of our sakes.

"Again, what can I do for you?" She uncrossed her arms and leafed through the stack of pink phone messages at her fingertips.

"Actually I came to see what I might do for you," I said, taking a deep breath. "I know as a professional it can be difficult being a newcomer to Green."

"I haven't found it difficult at all."

"Not at all?"

"I'm here to do a job, and that's what I do."

"So have you found a place to live?" I plowed on.

"I have leased an adequate condo on the lake." She looked at her expensive watch again. "Are you going somewhere with these questions? I'm on a tight schedule."

My reporter instincts kicked in, and I dug around in my leather handbag, a classy hand-me-down from Kevin. I pulled out a notebook and pen.

"For the record, what am I missing?" The question popped out of my mouth before I had thought it through. It rattled her even more than it surprised me.

"Could you reword that question?" She moved behind the desk and sat in a fake leather chair slightly larger than mine. "I don't understand what you're asking."

That makes two of us.

"I wonder what brought you to Green, a small school in a shrinking town. I notice you have strong education credentials and have worked in Texas."

"I'm an administrator. I get results in the school districts where I work."

"Districts? So you move around a lot?"

"I was an outstanding classroom teacher," she said, holding up a brass paperweight that apparently went with the framed award certificate on the wall. "I've been promoted for putting my classroom talents and my leadership skills to work for the good of students."

"I'm sorry." I mimicked her earlier words, "Could you repeat that? You lost me at classroom talents . . ."

The thrill of digging set in, and my defensiveness evaporated. She had moved up quickly, so she must be smart, ruthless, one very focused person, or some combination of the three. There was definitely a story here.

For the next twenty minutes, we sparred, me poking and prodding and receiving answers that sounded like something from an educational supply catalogue. The fun came when she accidentally let small facts slip, like when she described her "rise to education management."

"My father said, 'Prissy, you have proven yourself to be an example of excellence, and you should not hide that under a bushel.'" She managed a look that was half proud, half sensitive daughter.

"Prissy? You go by Prissy?"

"That was a long time ago. Now if you'll excuse me, I have another appointment."

I stood and walked to the window. A group of students of various races, about eighth- or ninth-graders, played basketball on the cracked court, no net on the rim. "How would you describe the demographics of our schools, Miss Robinson?"

"The demographics?" She frowned. "You know the community."

"I'd like to know your viewpoint as an academic outsider."

"The students, what few there are, are poor minorities," she said. "They are at risk in every statistical way possible, and need special attention."

I deliberately wrote slowly and repeated her quotes to her. "At risk," I said, picking up my purse. "I wonder if they've realized that yet."

The student worker knocked on the door and pushed it open wider. "Miss Robinson, you have another guest."

"Thank you, Mandy," she said, and the girl walked out.

"It's Randi," I corrected. "Not Mandy. She's named for her father, who was killed serving in the military in the Middle East before she was born."

"I stand corrected," she said and held out her hand to shake, demonstrating impressive hand-strength as she squeezed. She might be slight, but she was strong.

The man waiting for her, in a suit and tie, was seated in a brown metal folding chair and stood as I exited. My eyes widened despite my efforts to appear nonchalant.

"Come in, Dr. Hillburn," she said. "Ms. Craig was just leaving."

4

*One injury was reported at the Castor Spring Fling,
according to neighbors at the town park. A Little Rock
woman, running to catch up with her sister, slipped on
horse manure ignored by an equestrian group and
broke her wrist. The bluegrass concert afterwards,
however, was delightful.*

—*The Green News-Item*

Iris Jo stuck her head out of the newspaper conference room, her face serious.

"Lois, could you join us for a minute?" She fidgeted with her small gold chain in the way that Tammy often did with her chunky necklaces.

Puzzled, I set aside the office supply catalogue I was looking at and followed her to the door.

"Did I forget someone's birthday?" I whispered when I saw Tammy, Linda, and Stan already in the room, a box of Southern Girl doughnuts on the table.

"Not this time," Iris said, not quite able to meet my eyes. She took a seat next to Stan, a calendar open nearby. Linda glanced down at the file folder in front of her. Stan ran his ink-stained fingers around the neck of his jumpsuit. Tammy sat with her hands clasped in front of her, a camera nearby as always.

"We need to talk," Linda blurted out.

"What's going on?" I looked back at Iris, who kept *The Green News-Item* running day in and day out. I remained standing. "Has the financial situation gotten worse?"

"What's gotten worse is you," Tammy interrupted. "You're not acting like yourself."

The statement hit the room hard, and was heavier than one of the big chairs arranged around the oversized table. I looked from one face to the other of my staff of four. I felt as though I were onstage and couldn't remember my lines.

"Like right now," Tammy went on. "You're not saying anything. You always say something."

"Tammy," Iris murmured, "give Lois a moment to collect herself."

Stan stood and pulled back one of the heavy chairs. Without speaking, Linda handed me a cup of coffee, and Iris placed a glazed doughnut on a napkin in front of me.

I looked around the room, trying to avoid the seats that Tom, Katy, and Alex had always taken. "If someone doesn't tell me what's going on here, my head is going to explode."

"Now that's more like it," Tammy muttered, and Iris threw her a motherly "be quiet" look.

"We're approaching the end of January." Iris lifted the calendar as though it were a piece of evidence in a trial. "We haven't discussed what we're doing this year."

"We want to talk about where we're headed," Tammy said.

Linda pointed to the wood and brass plaque on the conference room wall, engraved with the newspaper's name and "Award of Excellence" in large letters. "We've got to live up to our reputation, or they might take our award back."

"We used to not think about stuff like this, but that all changed when you waltzed through that front door three years ago," Tammy continued.

"I did not waltz," I said. "I never waltz."

JUDY CHRISTIE

"We're planning our news coverage the day before, which doesn't work." Linda stood up and leaned against the wall. "We missed a school board meeting last week and didn't get photos of that accident on the highway construction site."

"When you flounder, we flounder," Tammy said.

"You're not exactly floundering," Iris said, "but we hope things can get back to normal."

There was that word *normal* again. "I thought things were going well." I felt as though my old friend Marti from Ohio had slapped me or that my beloved former boss Ed had reprimanded me.

"I told you this would hurt her feelings," Tammy said, looking at the others.

I had to get out of there before I started crying. I pointedly looked at my watch. "Right now I've got to drive out to Route Two to meet the builder. Apparently there's some sort of electrical problem. Unless I *flounder* during that meeting, I'll be back later."

I wrestled the big chair back, feeling my face flush as red as one of Mr. Sepulvado's summer tomatoes.

Tammy groaned, and Linda gave an uncharacteristic sigh. The uneasiness within me was reflected in their eyes.

"We want to help," Iris said softly.

"Thank you," I said, and hurried out, grabbing Holly Beth and my purse.

"That didn't go very well," Tammy said before I was out of earshot.

I nearly ran to my car, thankful I couldn't hear what else they had to say.

"Give me wisdom," I whispered, falling back on one of the first prayers I had uttered when I moved to Green.

A dozen dirty work trucks of various sizes lined the driveway and the road near our house. Most had business names painted on the sides and tools propped in the back. In one way or another, Chris and I were paying for all of them at this moment.

On a regular day that made me nervous, and after the meeting at work, it made me downright queasy.

The big dogs were in the fenced area in the back and jumped with excitement at my mid-day appearance, their barks mingling with hammering and an electric saw. Holly Beth gleefully romped with them when I opened the gate and placed her in the backyard.

Pausing to look at the house, I absorbed its dignity in the midst of the construction noise and longed for the day it would be a quiet haven.

"It has great bones, doesn't it?" Rick, the building contractor, interrupted my daydreams about refinishing the antique door and the baskets of flowers I planned to hang on the porch. "We've got a ways to go, but this has to be the best house I've ever worked on."

Turning to the sawhorses and array of tools, I nodded. "It's a special place, but I confess that rebuilding is harder than I anticipated."

"Mind if I give you some advice, Lois?" he asked.

With effort, I held my groan. "Why not?" I replied. "Seems like everyone else is."

"I'll tell you what I tell all my customers. Enjoy the remodeling, or you'll be miserable. Use the process to demonstrate what the house means to you." His smile took the sting from his words. "It's a choice."

His face was red, whether from the words or the cold I wasn't sure, and he referred to his clipboard and yelled for a young electrician, who scooted out from under the house, wearing an insulated jumpsuit and gloves.

"It's a mess under there." The man wiped mud off his face, sweating despite the cold day. "But we'll get you fixed up. We need to confirm where you want the plugs."

Not for the first time I wished Chris could get away from work during the day. He was much better at this kind of thing, and it felt good to lean on him.

Suddenly I realized that was what my staff had been trying to express a few minutes ago. They could take care of things themselves, but they liked it better when I led the way.

Before I could move, two workmen walked up. "While you're here, Miss Lois, can you take a look at the back bathroom wall?" a plumber asked. "We've found some rot in there."

Rick gave me a sympathetic look. "It's one of those things we couldn't plan for."

"How much will it slow us down?" I asked.

"Probably a week or so."

"Will it cost extra?"

"We'll work with you and Chris on it, but it's definitely going to take more manpower and materials."

I resisted the urge to stomp my foot. A pair of cardinals flitted through the bare branches of a tree by the driveway, and I took a deep breath. "We knew this was going to be a trial, didn't we?"

Rick looked down at his clipboard and hesitated. "It's a big job, but there won't be another place like this anywhere. We may ask more questions than those reporters of yours, but this home will have Lois and Chris stamped all over it."

"Enjoy the process, right?" I asked, noticing how the female cardinal's beak looked bright orange against a brown limb.

The contractor smiled. "Now we need answers on the sheetrock texturing and what y'all decided about windows."

Walking through our makeshift living quarters, I slipped through a giant sheet of plastic and could see my breath in the cold room. I pulled a notebook out of my purse, scanning notes and plans, answering questions, and jotting topics to discuss with Chris.

The remodeling chaos amazed me. But the work was somehow coming together despite the lack of any outward connection between workers and their varied projects. A worker tacked molding in one area, while another hammered wood to repair an arch between rooms. A carpenter in overalls and a flannel shirt was pulling off baseboards, his back to me, and I winced at the sound of the crowbar as the old wood came loose.

"That's prep work," Rick said, nodding toward the noise. "The trim guys will transform it into a work of art. You have to tear some of it out before you can fix it."

"That'll be nice," I said, trusting that he knew what the heck he was talking about.

"Luckily you got the roof done before all this rain," Rick said, seeming to sense my emotions. "That green tin looks great, and we can take care of the rest as long as we're in the dry. You've made it past the hard part."

⊶⊷

Trying to be thankful we had made it past the hard part —*yeah, right*—I left with a longer list of problems than I had arrived with and pulled my little car onto Route Two. I headed toward town, planning to stop at Pastor Jean's for a quick visit. A moment passed before I remembered I was going the wrong way.

Iris and Stan had postponed their house project down the road, staying at Stan's small house in town for now. A giant blue tarp covered Iris Jo's roof, and the oak that had fallen across the house was stacked into neat rows of firewood in the side yard.

Jean didn't live on Route Two anymore. The old church was gone, sold to the highway department. A crew of workmen had finished the demolition that the tornado had begun. The former parsonage was now a temporary highway office and storage shed.

The familiar corner where the church had stood had been bulldozed and graded, and the highway had taken shape, piles of red dirt smoothed into lanes, cement already poured on some of them. The former site of Chris's mobile home held a mound of gravel.

I turned around at the intersection, the beep-beep-beeping of heavy machinery in the background. Holly Beth gave a sharp, excited bark, almost as though she knew we were headed back toward home. She whined when I continued past our drive.

Rick stood in the yard, clipboard under his arm, and gave a wave. The worker in the overalls walked toward the driveway, crowbar in hand, his bent head covered in an orange stocking cap. He seemed vaguely familiar, and I tried to place him.

Pastor Jean's new parsonage was around the corner a couple of miles, across the road from the new Grace Chapel site. The church had bought the pastor a small brick home from a family who had moved to Shreveport, eager to get away from Green after the tornado.

"We've decided against raising our children out here in the country," the father had told Chris. "We want them to have opportunities we never did."

The remark had disturbed Chris.

"I've always enjoyed living in the country," he said as we walked one evening. "Do you think we're missing out?"

"Of course not. We're right where we need to be."

As I looked around the countryside today, still in the grip of a chilly winter, I pondered the question and was happy to see Jean's car in the driveway of the parsonage. I tapped on the door, Holly Beth under my coat, and stepped in when Jean responded.

"What a great surprise," she said, drying her hands on an embroidered towel. "Have you had lunch?"

When I shook my head, she began pulling out her usual stash of food in an assortment of plastic containers. Over meat loaf and a congealed salad that a church member had dropped by, Jean chatted about the Grace building project and unpacking in her new home. Sitting at the familiar kitchen table, I felt disoriented, looking for the window over the sink, where it had been in her other house.

"How do you do it?" I stabbed a marshmallow covered in something that tasted like lemon pudding. "You've nearly got the church built, and this place is already home. Chris and I are months from being settled."

"Unlike you, I didn't lose everything." She tapped the brightly colored Fiestaware cup. "I still have my old favorites." The kitchen, with its green Formica countertop and bright yellow flooring, had a peaceful feel, and I longed for my old kitchen, which had disappeared into the wind.

"I constantly have to remind myself that you and the church moved around the corner," I said. "To recall that my cottage blew away, that Tom is dead, that I need fresh ideas for the *News-Item*."

"Our minds have a tough time keeping up, don't they?" she said. "Those state counselors said big traumas take years to get over."

"I hoped it'd be more like months." I leaned over and patted Holly, who had curled up in Jean's lap. "So many things are good in my life. I shouldn't whine."

"I wish I had the perfect words for you, Lois, but I don't. I miss the old parsonage and the church building . . . but we can't go back. . . ."

"So we move forward together," I said, recalling a scripture we had discussed with the children who came to church on Wednesday nights. "That's why we have other people to lean on. If one of us falls down, another can help us up."

She sat quietly, allowing me time to sort my thoughts, a gift she had.

"Abundant life," I said finally. "We choose whether to be miserable or happy."

"That sounds like a good topic for a sermon," Jean replied.

"I learned it from a carpenter." An odd look washed over her face, and I laughed when it dawned on me what she was thinking. "Not *that* carpenter. Rick, our contractor."

The pastor, a somewhat reserved woman by nature, hooted in laughter. "Oh, Lois, doesn't God speak to us in the strangest ways?"

The sound of her delight took away my rough edges, the way I smoothed surfaces at our house with sandpaper, and I chuckled, my gloomy mood lifted. "If there's one thing I've learned in Green, it's that things have a way of working out," I said.

An advantage of a small staff was the short time it took to round everyone up for a meeting.

"You're right," I said, when we gathered in the newsroom later that day, the smell of burnt popcorn coming from the nearby microwave. "We need an investigative project with an editorial crusade."

"Let's choose a topic," Linda said, a look of excitement unusual for her on her face.

"How about the new highway?" Tammy asked. "The bypass should open later this year, and it'll change Green forever. Think of how many people won't even come downtown anymore."

"But everyone knows the bypass is coming, and we've done dozens of updates," Linda said.

"So you're saying that's a story for further on down the road?" Tammy asked, preening at her pun. Everyone laughed.

"This feels almost like the way things used to be," Molly said, setting her soft drink down and looking every bit the college coed in her jeans and scoop-necked shirt. An African-American student from a poor family, she was making all A's in her first year in college.

"Let's do a story about schools," she suggested. "Anthony said some guy in a suit is hanging out at Green High and told Mr. Ellis our school isn't very good, the same thing Miss Robinson said that day I went to pick up my sister."

"I'm hearing the same reports," Linda said, "from my sources at the courthouse and the School Board office."

Each person on the tiny staff nodded.

"Let's get started," I said.

5

Briarwood Baptist Tabernacle asks for ideas as members wrestle with questions about the future of the church. Deacon Jimmy Joe Jones said, "Everything was going fine until we started talking about what color carpet to put in our sanctuary. Nearly split the church." Mr. J.J. stressed that his church is full of good people, but "we all know everyone has strong opinions about decorating."

—The Green News-Item

Chris stood at the sink gulping down a bowl of cereal. His customary glass of orange juice was nowhere in sight.

"What're you thinking about?" I asked as I poured my first cup of coffee of the day.

My voice almost seemed to surprise him. "The usual," he said. "About my classes, what I'm teaching today." He set the dish down with such force I thought it might crack.

"You seem rushed." Most days I could set my watch by Chris's prework schedule, but today he was at least thirty minutes ahead and acted almost brooding.

"There's a lot going on at work."

"Are you still having extra meetings?" I shook cereal into a bowl and pulled the milk out of the refrigerator.

"Is this a breakfast visit or an interview?" he snapped. I was so stunned, I sloshed milk onto the counter.

"I'm sorry," he said quickly. "I'm tired, and we have an early faculty meeting."

"Before school? What's up with that?"

He shook his head and reached for his jacket. "They didn't say, but I'd better go or Priscilla Robinson will put a black mark by my name. She's pretty hard on the teachers."

I walked a few steps across the kitchen and gave him a fierce hug. I loved this man so much that some days it felt like my heart might burst with the happiness of it. "You're doing too much. You coach, lead practices, teach, take good care of me, do more than your share of the work on our house."

"Sounds like someone else I know." He gave me a gentle kiss on the lips, almost as though comforting me, and looked at the hand-me-down clock over the sink. "I'd better run. See you at the game?"

I nodded and waved as he drove off, his pickup sounding like it could fall apart at any minute on the bumpy gravel road. Maybe I'd suggest again that he buy a new one.

My husband's odd behavior made me feel off-balance. I liked him to be steady and predictable, making up for my erratic days at the *Item*.

———

When I walked into the newspaper lobby, Tammy stood behind the counter, both palms flat down on the Shreveport paper, reading. Her purse and insulated lunch box still sat on the counter, next to other out-of-town papers in their plastic sacks.

"Morning," I said and started to scoot through to my office. I hoped she wasn't in one of her chatty moods.

She looked up before I could take another step, her face pale. "Have you heard?"

My heart jumped into my throat, and the names of the many people I loved in Green ran through my mind. I stopped in front of the counter, putting an impatient Holly Beth on the floor.

"Did someone get hurt?" I thought of Aunt Helen, my mentor who died my first year in Green, and Tom, who perished in the tornado. "Or die?"

Tammy shook her head. "This." She tapped a headline on the "Regional Roundup" page with her pink nail and turned the paper toward me. "The state wants to close our school."

"What?" I snatched the page so quickly that the corner tore. "There must be some mistake."

"They're going to merge all our grades with other schools."

I read the headline out loud. "State Studies Low-Performing School in Green."

Tammy didn't wait for me to continue. "A team has been hired to make recommendations for where kids will go and how the transition will work."

Still reading, I bumped my leg on the latched gate at the counter. Tammy reached over, released the latch, and held the gate for me.

Propping myself against my office doorframe, I let my purse and leather tote bag slip to the floor, and Tammy stood next to me as I read the article out loud. Quotes from "Texas consultant Marcus Hillburn" were sprinkled throughout.

"Chris is going to be heartbroken," I said.

Linda burst in at that moment with a large paper cup and her canvas bag, always full of notebooks, pens, a dictionary, a paperback novel, pretzels, and who-knew-what-else. She started talking the second she opened the door. "It's all over town that the Green school is about to shut down. We've been scooped in our own backyard."

I was so stiff that I might as well have been glued to the wall.

"The Shreveport paper broke the story, and now they're reporting it on the Alexandria television station," she said.

My mind felt like it had once when I had a bad case of the flu, stuffy and muddled. I tried to decide which question to ask first. "How could they think our school is bad?"

"Bureaucratic idiots," Tammy said. "Out-of-town consultants who think they have it all figured out."

"None of that matters at the moment," Linda said. "Today is Tuesday. We've got to write this story before eleven o'clock. This is a disaster, and it's my fault. I should have worked my beat better."

"Don't beat yourself up," I said. I lived with one of the key sources and had missed the story under my nose.

"They say they're working on a tight timeline and plan to send students to other schools by fall," Tammy said. "I need to call Walt and see if this is legal."

I grabbed the phone out of her hand. "Everyone take a deep breath. This is a major story, and we need a plan to cover it fast."

Picking up my purse and bag, I moved into my office, calling over my shoulder, "Linda, see if you can find Molly. Tammy, go to the press room and warn Stan that we'll be pushing the deadlines for today's paper. Ask him to call Iris Jo at her doctor's appointment and tell her what's going on."

Turning my computer on, I found the e-mail from the Department of Education, a news release that had come late the previous day.

"Because of inaction of local authorities, we have been forced to step in," an assistant secretary of something said. Full of bureaucratic language and doublespeak, it boiled down to one thing: Green was too small to support its own school.

Students would be bused to consolidated schools in other communities.

The document outlined research done "by national experts in the field of education," including more convoluted quotes from Mayor Hillburn's ex-husband.

The press release ended with a quote from the person described as "New Executive Principal and Transition Coordinator, Priscilla Robinson."

"This efficient solution will not only save taxpayers money, but help students get the best education possible with the dollars available," she said, announcing a "change of role" for long-time principal Eugene Ellis. He would assume the role of Assistant Principal/Discipline "to spend more time with his family." A quote from Eugene was conspicuously absent.

I threw the newspaper across the room, and Holly Beth barked and ran to it, picking it up in her mouth, growling, and shaking it as though she were as angry as I was.

Knowing Chris was in class, I tried his cell phone, which went straight to voice mail. A combination of anger and worry clashed within my heart and mind. I wondered how much he knew about the impending change and worried about how this would hit him. "Calling to see how you are," I said. "Call when you can. Love you. Bye."

I tried the school office, but the line was busy. No doubt everyone in town was calling. This news probably flew around town faster than Marcus and Pearl Taylor's patio furniture in the tornado.

Re-reading the release, I hit the print button on my computer and made a half-dozen copies of the e-mail, scarcely believing the way Marcus Hillburn had snarled about Green and the way Priscilla had made it sound like closing the school was actually a gift to the community.

Iris Jo rushed in as I made a list of story ideas and questions. "I cancelled my appointment as soon as I heard," she said. "Tell me someone has their wires crossed."

"They've got their wires crossed, all right."

"If they kill our school, they'll kill our community," Iris said. "How are we going to stop them?"

Within minutes the staff had gathered, even Molly. "I was driving to class and heard it on the radio. I couldn't sit through a history lecture with this on my mind."

"You shouldn't skip," I said. "College courses are hard enough to keep up with as it is."

"I wouldn't be sitting here today if it weren't for the Green school." She sounded like Katy, an unusual passion in her voice. "We can't let this happen."

"We may not have a choice," Linda said.

"If we explain it, maybe they'll see how wrong they are. I'm only eighteen, and I see how stupid this is. Surely they will too."

"We definitely have to try," I said. "We're playing catch-up, though."

Linda picked up her reporter's notebook and read from a list that mirrored mine. "We need photos, local reaction, and the state update." Watching her grow as a journalist made my throat grow tight, as did Molly's next words.

"I miss Tom," Molly said. "He'd be all over this story."

"We wouldn't have gotten scooped if Tom were alive," Linda said. "He would have heard about this before the rest of the world. He had that knack."

She was right.

I pictured him driving out to my wedding to warn us about the tornado and realized anew the hole his death left.

"We'll figure out later how we let this slip by," I said. "Now we've got to tell readers how it affects their lives. That public relations puff piece tries to make it sound like a done deal, but it's ambiguous."

"We'll investigate how far along it is and what might stop it," Linda said.

"Our community correspondents can contact neighbors for quotes," Tammy said, "and I'll head to the school to shoot pictures."

"Someone needs to write an editorial," Iris said.

All four heads turned to me, like the synchronized swimming competition during the Olympics. If I hadn't been so tense, it would have been comical.

"I'm awfully close to this story," I said.

Tammy snorted. "What story are you not close to? You're up to your eyeballs in everything that happens in Green. If anyone can make it right, you can."

"I know one thing," I said. "We're not going to let them take our school without giving it our best shot."

———

Unable to get through by phone, Linda headed to the school for comments. The new principal's response suggested the newspaper had a fierce battle on its hands, the fate of the school to be the prize.

"She gave me a two-line statement and forbids faculty and staff to talk to the media," Linda said.

"Leave it to her to give her two-sentences worth," Tammy quipped. "I've about had it up to here with outsiders coming in and telling us what to do." She glanced at me. "Present company excluded."

By midmorning, the town was in a fury. People who hadn't had a child in school in decades demanded the *News-Item* do something. Parents were hysterical and called the newspaper by the dozens. Businesses were alarmed, and leaders from Green Forward, South Green Merchants Group, and the Lakeside Neighborhood Association set up emergency meetings and urged the newspaper to "make sure this closing doesn't go through."

"We can't have a community without a school," the garden club president said, stopping by with a bouquet of variegated camellias in a jelly jar. "Everyone in my family graduated from Green High."

"Our 4-H students will quit the program if they go to school so far away," Bud said, stopping by with Anna Grace. "They already have to get up before daylight to take care of their animals."

"This will hurt poor students whose parents can't drive them to school," Mr. Marcus, Kevin's father, said, representing the Lakeside neighborhood organization. "We'll take a step back in bringing our community together."

Chris called before his early lunch shift. "So you heard the news," he said. "Are you OK?"

"The question is, are *you* OK? I've been so worried about you."

"It doesn't seem possible, does it?"

I caught my breath at the sadness in his voice. "What are you hearing on campus?" I asked.

"I can't talk right now." His voice dropped. "Needless to say, things are in an uproar around here."

"You already knew, didn't you?" The hurt mixed with anger and anxiety made my voice wobble. "Why didn't you say anything?"

"I didn't know anything but the endless rumors that have flown around the past couple of days." He spoke so quietly I could barely hear him. "I hoped it would go away before you got drawn into it."

"If you had told me, the *Item* wouldn't have been scooped by our competition."

"I'm sorry the *Item* paper didn't have it first. I know that matters a lot to you. But I wasn't sure it was true. You know how gossip spreads around here, and I didn't want to get you worked up if it was nothing."

He bit into the apple he had packed with his lunch. I could hear him chewing. My frustration with bureaucrats who didn't care about Green transferred to Chris, which even I knew wasn't logical. I couldn't stop my words. "Didn't I deserve to hear the rumors, since I run the community newspaper and you work at the school?"

"Lois, when I left school yesterday, no one knew what was going on. I thought you'd probably get the information before I did. I don't like being in the middle of this." He sounded annoyed, although he was almost whispering. "It feels like one student tattling on another."

"But you're married to a journalist," I said.

"So I noticed."

"A hint would have been nice."

"I know this is a big deal to the paper," he said, "and I know you'll do your best with it. It's difficult enough as it is, without you and me arguing over it."

My head spun. In my years of fantasies about marriage, I never imagined being at odds with my husband over a story, him on one side, me on the other.

"We have to report on this," I said.

The sound of him wadding up the paper lunch sack crackled in my ear. "I know that, and you know I will support you in any way I can. You do your job, and I'll do mine."

"I don't want to fight," I said. "Is Priscilla running around campus thumping her chest?"

"It's like someone hit a yellowjacket nest around here. I've never seen so much buzzing around in my life."

"Do you think it'll happen—that they'll close the school?"

"Looks like it'd take an Act of Congress to stop this now." I heard a noise in the background, and Chris spoke to someone else before coming back to the phone.

"I've been assigned extra cafeteria duty, so I'd better go. I don't want to get fired for talking to the press." His laugh sounded forced. "Miss Robinson and I aren't exactly on the best of terms, and she's running the show. My job could be on the line."

"Whatever happens, we're in it together," I said. "I love you way more than this newspaper or that school."

"Me too," he said. "See you tonight."

The editorial was easy to write.

I pictured graduates like Katy and Molly, students like Anthony, and toddlers like Asa who would be deprived of something special if the school closed. Ignoring my desire to blast every bureaucrat from Bouef Parish to Baton Rouge, I chose Tom's classic approach, explaining how real people, businesses, and the future of Green would be damaged.

I asked local citizens and leaders to let their voices be heard.

My phone conversation with James Spurlock, superintendent of schools, Katy's stepdad, and fellow member of Grace Community Chapel, was unsatisfying.

"This hurts me as much as it hurts the rest of the town," he said, "but we've fought as long as we can. The state took the decision out of our hands. We don't have enough students—or enough money— to keep the school open."

"Then why can't the other schools merge with us?" I asked.

"I've been over that with you already," he said, exasperation in his voice. "Those facilities are newer and cost less to maintain."

"Can't you at least propose a different approach? This will change Green forever—and not for the better."

"I'm responsible for the entire parish," he said. "I have to look out for all the students, not merely the ones in town. I thought I had a solution worked out, but that consultant took exception to it. It all comes down to the bottom line."

"Students matter more than money." I almost sputtered the words, and James sighed.

"I agree. But we can't spend money we don't have. Dr Marcus Hillburn is the country's preeminent school-merger expert, and what he says will stand."

"Will it help if I talk to him?"

"Between you and me, it's like talking to a brick wall." A telephone rang in the background. "I need to go. I'm sorry, Lois. I'll e-mail you an official response in a few minutes."

After a brief phone visit with Mayor Eva, I announced on page one that the *Item* would coordinate a letter-writing campaign and a town meeting. "The school is the glue that holds our community together," I wrote. "Green has been tested before and made the grade. We must not fail this time."

I shouldn't have been shocked when Major Wilson made a collect call from prison to the newspaper. Tammy was out shooting photographs, so I picked up the receiver and listened to the recorded message asking if I would take the call. For a brief moment I considered hanging up, but Major, for all his flaws, had loaned Chris and me his travel trailer to live in when our house blew away.

So I took the call. "Even jail can't keep you out of the loop, can it, sir?"

"You know I don't like being called 'sir,' and I don't think much of your operation there," he said. "But every town needs some sort of newspaper and a school. I figure if anybody can stop this nonsense, it's you and my sister. She got elected mayor because of those smarts of hers, and you're no dummy, either."

That was the closest to a compliment he'd ever paid me.

"And your point is?" I was thinking of how much the call would cost my weak newspaper budget and the busy schedule ahead.

"Go to the legislature. Call the governor. Don't let an outsider come in and tell the town what to do. Rally the troops."

Mayor Eva was glad to see me when I visited her office on the second floor of the courthouse, a small room she rarely used, preferring her well-decorated office at her department store.

"I've had so many calls today that I moved over here," she said. "So much for this being a part-time job."

"I heard from your brother," I said.

Her eyes narrowed. "I told him not to call you anymore, but I suppose he can't resist sticking his nose in this one."

"He says you and I can block this."

She crossed her arms on the desk. With her knit suit, perfect hair, and elegant jewelry, she looked like the chairwoman of the board of a major corporation, transforming the sterile office into a seat of power. I had seen that look on her face many times. She meant business.

"I don't know if we can prevent it," she said, picking up her expensive pen, a Christmas gift from her old friend and my former enemy Dub McCuller. "But, as always, we have to work hard to make this right."

The school gym was packed at tip-off time for the basketball game. The sport always drew a crowd, one of the few places the entire community gathered, and tonight many non-regular fans had shown up, too. Several people held posters that said things like "Save Our Schools" and "Green Rabbits Rule 4Ever."

A student I didn't know passed out bright yellow sheets of paper, and I noticed Executive Principal Priscilla Robinson trying to stop him but being blocked by a line of parents.

"Members of Save Our School will meet at 5 p.m. next Tuesday in the school parking lot," the sheet read, quoting Brent Fish as SOS Chair. "We want the Bouef Parish School Board to hear us out. That board needs to know we can't be ignored." I folded a copy and put it in my pocket, wincing that we had been scooped again, this time by a community group and a copy machine.

From my usual perch, I looked around the gym, missing Kevin, who was on call, and Molly, who was working at her other job at the Pak-N-Go. Chris looked up and waved, and I could tell even from a distance how tired he was. Mr. Ellis, usually pumping hands in the crowd, sat to himself on the end of the bottom row. He was not wearing his usual Green Rabbits shirt.

Priscilla Robinson, or "Miss Priss," as Tammy had started calling her, took the microphone before the game. Its perpetual squealing partially covered the boos and hisses.

I squirmed, embarrassed at what the visiting team from a school in the next parish must think about us. Despising the new administrator was one thing, but Green's reputation for having nice people was on the line.

"Ladies and gentleman," Priscilla said. When no one seemed to hear her, she started over, but the restless crowd would not quiet down.

Chris stood near the bench where the players sat, and ran his finger around the collar of his coach's shirt. He stepped out on the court and held up both hands.

"Friends," he said in a loud voice, and the crowd immediately quieted. "Let's give Miss Robinson our attention and get this game started."

The new principal started again, as though her coach hadn't said anything. "This is our first gathering since the unsettling news this morning, and I want to tell you how sorry I am that you are upset that your school is to be closed."

The crowd began to heat up again. My husband, who had stayed next to her, once more raised a hand for silence.

"We will do everything we can to make this a smooth transition," she said, "and will depend on each of you to help."

"Not going to happen," a man yelled.

"Go back where you came from," a woman next to me in a Green High sweatshirt called out.

The sound caught Priscilla's attention, and she looked up at me, anger in her eyes. *Surely she didn't think I'd said that?* Those same words had been thrown at me way too often in the early months in Green.

"Let's play basketball," she said. "Good luck to both teams."

She returned to the stands and sat next to Marcus Hillburn, who patted her knee with a smirk. Mr. Ellis got up and walked out.

6

Green Lanes Bowling Center reports the locker renova-
tion project is nearing completion. New keys will be
issued in time for Spring Leagues. We have unclaimed
equipment that can't be identified, so see Emma Jane at
the front desk, and label your gear before leaving it for
extended periods. Green Lanes knows there are several
league bowlers who are still missing balls and
asks for your patience.

—*The Green News-Item*

Tammy and Walt had tried to get Chris and me to their house for dinner for months.

"You keep saying there's not enough time to go around, but that's silly," Tammy said, flopping into her favorite chair in my office. "You have plenty of time to do what you want to do, and I think you don't want to come see us."

"That's ridiculous. You know we have the house and the school situation and so much to do at the *Item*, and that's a long drive at night."

"It's fifty miles each way, the same distance it is every day when I come and go at the paper."

"It's a busy time," I said again.

"Last fall you couldn't visit because of your house hunt and tornado recovery and Katy and Alex moving off." Tammy was in all-out fighting mode, and in her sleek black pants outfit, she looked a little like a Ninja warrior. "There'll always be something. If you don't want to come, say so."

Discussing it with Chris later, I was forced to admit there was some truth to Tammy's words. "I'm not sure I can bear to see their beautiful new home yet. Our house is so chaotic."

I ran one hand down my overalls and swept my other hand around the room. "If we have company, they have to sit on a couch in the room where we sleep. No one has lived in Tammy's place before, while we have spiderwebs dating back to the turn of the century."

Chris scooted next to me on the couch, salvaged from his youngest brother's storage shed. "Lois, we didn't want a new house, remember?"

"Good point." I lifted Holly Beth, so spoiled she didn't like to jump up on the sofa on her own. "You know I'm happy for them, right?"

"We ought to pay Walt and Tammy a visit. It'll be a nice break for us."

"And it'll make Tammy so happy to share her home with us after that garage apartment where she used to live. She keeps saying she doesn't deserve to live so high on the hog."

"Her parents weren't very nice people," Chris said. "My father, who never says a mean word about anyone, did farming business with them years ago and said he was happy to see the back of them."

"Tammy won't talk about that with me, even after more than three years. Even though she looks out for me like a sister who needs protecting from bullies, I can't get her to open up about herself."

"You've done a lot for her," Chris said, "letting her take pictures and giving her part ownership of the *Item* . . ." He pulled me closer, much to Holly's annoyance. ". . . Choosing to marry me so she could have Walt."

"When you put it like that . . ." I leaned up for his kiss. "I'll get with her tomorrow and plan a visit."

———⌒∞⌒———

The stylish iron gate to the South Shreveport subdivision was closed when we pulled up, and neither Chris nor I could figure out the intercom system, punching in random numbers and disagreeing whether we were supposed to hit the # sign or the *.

My mind flashed back to my first day at *The Green News-Item*, when Tammy had been reluctant to let me in the front door before hours. "She's still locking me out," I grumbled.

Finally Chris hit the right button, and Walt's delighted voice welcomed us. "Tammy was beginning to think you'd never get here," he said.

The gate slid open after the right code was activated, and we wound through an upscale neighborhood, with every yard mowed and edged, purple pansies in most flower beds, and cute seasonal flags fluttering near porch lights, some for Mardi Gras, others with hearts for Valentine's Day.

Tammy and Walt, looking every bit the yuppie newlyweds, held hands in their doorway as we pulled into their drive, and a smile lit Tammy's face as she rushed toward the car.

"I'm sorry you had trouble getting in," she said. "Half the time that gate doesn't work right. It's not very welcoming."

Walt, whom I had dated a handful of times when I first came to Green and who helped the newspaper with legal issues, seemed a bit sheepish about the security, too. "We wanted to live out this way so Tammy wouldn't have so far to drive to work. There weren't many houses available."

He shook hands with Chris and gave me a hug. "Tammy's got appetizers to tide us over until dinner."

"They're really snacks," Tammy said, fidgeting with her necklace.

We followed them through a beautiful cypress door and a small tile foyer, into a large room with a fireplace made of old bricks and a gorgeous hardwood floor.

"Home sweet home," Tammy said, grabbing my hand. "What do you think?"

"It's beautiful," I said. My eyes couldn't take in all the features I loved, from the walls the color of café au lait to the subdued piece of original art over the mantel to the big windows lining the back wall.

"There's a beautiful view during the day," Tammy said, following my eyes. "Walt, why don't you get them something to drink, and I'll finish getting supper ready."

"Promise you'll give us the full tour after we eat?" I asked. "I want to see every inch."

"Sure," Tammy beamed. "I've been dying to see what you think."

My eyes widened when we walked into the kitchen, which made ours look like the worst "before" picture ever in a home makeover magazine. Tammy didn't seem to notice, slipping on an apron that said "Kiss the Cook" and pulling a glass bowl out of a top-of-the-line refrigerator.

"That's amazing," I said.

"It's just spinach with strawberries and pecans." She shrugged.

"I meant the fridge. And the stove, too, and the countertops . . . and that sink." I walked over to the soapstone sink and ran my hand over it. "If I didn't like you so much, I'd be jealous about your sink."

"Oh, Lois." Tammy laughed and handed me a stack of plates covered with flowers. "Shut up and set the table. Let's eat on the breakfast table. The dining room's a little formal, if you ask me."

Our conversation during the meal covered every topic from how to get grass to grow in the shade to how well Anthony had played during the most recent Rabbits basketball games to whether Kevin and Terrence were dating steadily.

"I've wanted to ask," Tammy said, "but last time I brought it up, she snapped at me like an alligator going after a piece of raw chicken."

"My wife not prying into other people's business?" Walt said with a grin. "What is the world coming to?"

"Isn't it the truth?" Chris said.

"You have to admit they make a good couple," I said.

Walt pushed back from the table. "I think that's the husbands' cue to look at the sound system in the den. You with me, Chris?"

Both men helped clear the table before they left the room, stacking the dishes loudly on the counter. Chris paused to look at both of us as they wandered off. "Try not to change the future of the Western world while we're gone."

Tammy protested when I started rinsing the dishes, but I went right ahead. "Teamwork," I said. "You load the dishwasher. It's how my mother-in-law and I do it."

Putting leftovers in the refrigerator, I stroked the smooth panel. "This is fantastic, and you have enough bins to store vegetables for a month. You planning on opening a restaurant?"

"Is it too big?" Tammy asked with the anxious note she got when a news photograph wasn't perfect in her eyes. "The appliance guy recommended it."

"There's no such thing as a too-big refrigerator," I said. "And your range even has a griddle. I've wanted one of those since I got out of college."

"That stove should've come with a warning," she said. "Now Walt and his parents want me to make pancakes every weekend. Isn't it weird that I live in a house like this?"

"There's not the slightest weird thing about it," I said. "May I offer a piece of advice?"

Her eyes widened. "You're scaring me. Since when do you ask me before you offer advice?"

I took both of her hands, damp from the sink, and looked her in the eyes. "Don't be afraid to be happy. Walt's a lucky guy to have found you."

For one rare moment, Tammy was speechless.

Then she smiled.

"When you knocked on that newspaper door way back when, I almost didn't let you in," she said. "Wouldn't that have been the biggest mistake of my life?"

Chris and Walt had settled into matching recliners in a small television room and were watching a college basketball game. They argued loudly with the call an official made and barely looked up as we walked into the room.

"Give me the grand tour," I said. "Something tells me the guys aren't budging for a while."

We chatted as we made our way through each room. I made mental notes on faucets, drawer pulls, and light fixtures, and thought about retrieving my remodeling notebook from my purse.

"This house has such an elegant feel to it." I ran my hand over a marble vanity in the guest bathroom.

"I know it's not cozy like your house will be," Tammy said. "I never dreamed I would live in a house this fancy."

We lingered upstairs in the guest room, where a small uphol-stered rocker complemented a headboard made of cherry. The matching dresser had a fancy oval mirror, and bedside tables held an assortment of knickknacks, including a small brass rabbit.

"My best friend gave that to me in eighth grade," Tammy said when I picked it up. "You know what they say. 'Once a Green Rabbit, always a Green Rabbit.'"

"That reminds me." I sat on the edge of the rocker. "Will you organize a Green Grads community page, with essays from Green High alums and photos of them at work? That can show the value of the school through the years."

Tammy looked almost wary, a totally foreign look for her face, as I continued. "Maybe get Kevin to write about how her science teacher made her want to be a doctor and Eva to talk about campaigning for sixth-grade class president."

She seemed to know what I was going to say next because she started shaking her head before I started.

"You can write about taking pictures for the yearbook and how being a Green Rabbit never goes away," I said.

"I'm not a writer," she said.

"I thought you'd be thrilled," I said. "You love doing things with the community."

"Let's go see what the menfolk are up to." She disappeared before I was even out of the room.

Tammy was eating a bag of M&M's when I walked into work Monday morning, a sure sign the week was off to a rough start.

"Crazy calls already?" I asked.

"Not yet," she said.

"So why the chocolate?"

"It's still early," she said. "I'm preparing myself."

"Chris and I had a great time Saturday. Your home is gorgeous. I hope you'll help when we get ready to decorate ours."

"You know I didn't do any of that. My taste isn't nearly that good."

I gave a snort that sounded like one of the regular sounds she made. "You may have hired someone, but she didn't come with all of that on her own. I saw your style everywhere."

"Really?" She brightened. "That's the same thing Walt says."

"So why don't you believe him?"

She fidgeted with her trademark clunky beads, today in hot pink, over a light pink sweater that looked like cashmere. "He always says nice things," she said. "He's way too good for me."

"Tammy! I thought you were over that craziness. The man adores you. You adore him. Enough said."

She shrugged. "We'll see."

During our staff meeting later, my idea for the Green Grads page got rave reviews from everyone but Tammy, who steered the conversation to Iris Jo's idea to run old school pictures sent in by readers.

"I'll gather those up," Tammy said, "and get the copy from grads. Linda, do you want to write a piece for us?"

I frowned. "Linda has her hands full. I hoped you'd do something."

"I told you I'm not a writer," she said and stomped out of the room.

"What was that all about?" Linda asked.

"Beats me."

When Tammy stuck her head in my office later, she looked like a repentant Katy, who occasionally let her emotions run away from her.

"Got a second?" Tammy asked.

I nodded and debated whether to move around the desk to sit next to her. I stayed put.

"I need to tell you why I don't want to write a piece for the Green Grads page," she said in a low voice. "I'd just as soon not tell everybody."

"I didn't mean to push so hard," I said. "I know everyone isn't cut out to be a writer."

"I can't write about being a graduate. I never graduated. Not from Green High or anywhere else."

For some, this admission might have been accompanied by a tear or a pained sigh, but Tammy crossed her arms and looked as though she might head butt me at any moment.

"I failed half my classes my senior year, and barely passed the other ones. They let me walk across the stage and get a blank piece of paper because I promised to go to summer school. I ran away from home instead."

Since that cold January day when I first walked up to the *News-Item*, Tammy had often flabbergasted me. She worked as hard as was needed, which around here was pretty hard. She had taught herself to be an excellent photojournalist, married a lawyer, pushed me when I didn't know I needed pushing, and always had my back. She would appear with an aspirin and a bottle of water before I even realized I had a headache.

This announcement surprised me in an altogether different way. I knew my next words would matter, and I quickly ruled out the kind response that might have worked for someone else.

"Looks like you found your way back," I said. "Probably just as well."

"I was a mess. I wanted to start over somewhere . . . any-where . . . I did the dumbest things."

"You were a kid. You've worked here since you were nineteen, so you must not have been gone long."

"I came back when I got out of jail."

"Jail?"

"I shoplifted an expensive ring over in Dallas." Before continuing she glanced down at the beautiful engagement ring Walt had given her.

"I was in jail for six months and had to pay them back. When I got out, my parents had moved to East Texas and didn't have any burning urge for me to live with them. The only place I knew to go was Green. I got a part-time job throwing papers, and after a while, Iris promoted me to front-desk clerk."

"Does she know?" I inclined my head toward Iris Jo's office.

"No one knows—except my parents, who I haven't heard from since they kicked me out. Oh, and a lenient judge who told me to straighten up and fly right."

"Does Walt know?" I asked haltingly.

She lowered her head, no longer looking cocky. "I couldn't bring myself to tell him when we started dating. Now it's too late."

I waited.

"He's a lawyer from a high-brow family. I'm a high-school dropout with a criminal record. My mother and father are losers from way back. You were the first person who ever truly believed in me."

"He strikes me as a forgiving sort of guy," I said. "Walt got me through more than one crisis. Don't you think you should tell him?"

"He ought to have a smart, classy wife." An uncommon tear ran down her face. "He's going to be so disappointed in me."

"I've seen the way he looks at you. Something tells me a diploma isn't going to change that."

"I love him so much, Lois. What am I going to do?"

I tried to think of what Chris or Pastor Jean might say. "What do you want to do?"

"I want to tell him the truth, and I want to get my GED, and I want to go to college, and I want to be a wife Walt can be proud of."

"Well, there's your answer."

—⦾⦾⦾—

After Tammy confessed to Walt, he immediately drove her to the bookstore to buy a General Education Development study guide and took her to her favorite restaurant for dinner.

"He said the degree only matters to him if it matters to me," she told me the next day, her look subdued but a glint of gratitude in her eyes.

Showing me her workbook and online materials, she began to smile. "Walt's right, as usual. I'm not only doing this for him. I'm doing it for myself."

Although Tammy was ashamed of her secret at first, the more she studied, the less it bugged her. By the end of the week, when Molly found her poring over a math worksheet at lunch in the newsroom, the chief photographer/clerk/new student gave her a big smile. "You're not the only scholar around this place," she said.

"Are you taking online college courses?" Molly looked puzzled.

"I'm doing something I should have done years ago."

As she explained about her misdeeds as a teen, Molly's eyes got big, and then an inquisitive look came to her face. "Is the test hard?"

"I think so," Tammy said. "I'm not going to take the actual exam for a few months because I need to study a lot more. I didn't do so great on the practice test."

"You've hardly started studying," I said. "Why did you take the practice test?"

She threw me one of her famous Tammy looks. "You would have done the same thing. I wanted to see where I stood."

Tammy knew me well. I'd have to know how far I had to go.

"Do you think anyone could pass it?" Molly asked.

"I don't see why not," Tammy said, "if they studied."

I wondered where my youngest employee was headed with her questions. "Do you have a friend who dropped out?" I asked.

"I'm thinking about my mother."

"Your mother didn't finish either?" Tammy looked almost excited.

"She dropped out of high school to have me. If she had her degree, she might be able to get a promotion at the nursing home."

"I'd be glad to help her," Tammy said. "In fact, she can have this. I can get another one." She held out her precious book.

"I don't know," Molly said. "She's embarrassed about it. She might not like me telling you."

"I felt the same way. Lois convinced me that working toward it is something to be proud of."

"I'll think about it," the girl said.

"They have all sorts of free materials at the library." The tone of Tammy's voice told how important she thought this was. Then she grinned. "Tell her Lois said she'd pay for the test itself."

"You have to pay?" I was stunned, not at subsidizing Molly's mother, Esther, but that people couldn't get their GED without a fee.

"They have to be graded and everything." Tammy shrugged. "It's about fifty bucks or so. Walt and I would be happy to help, too."

Iris Jo walked in during the last of the conversation and looked over Tammy's shoulder. "So you're finally going to finish high school?" she asked. "Good for you!"

"You knew?" Tammy's look was priceless.

"You listed yourself as a Green High graduate on your job application." Iris gave a small smile. "I made a phone call to follow up."

"Not much gets past Iris," I said, picking at the lettuce on my sandwich from the Cotton Boll.

"Sometimes I do better than others." Iris pulled a chair next to Molly, who almost always sat at Tom's old desk. "You're forgetting I let Lee Roy Hicks and Chuck McCuller nearly steal the newspaper blind. I can't brag about not letting things slip by."

The conversation meandered from Tammy's GED quest to the paper's past.

"Was Mr. Dub involved in that theft, too?" Molly asked.

"Somewhat," Iris said. "When all was said and done, he was mostly a victim of Chuck's manipulation."

"I'd hardly call Dub McCuller anybody's victim," Tammy said. "He came out smelling like a rose." She reached over and grabbed one of my potato chips.

"He paid a big fine," Iris said, "and Eva sure seems to like him. Joe Sepulvado's staying with him until he gets back on his feet, so I guess Dub's not all bad."

"Do you think Mr. Dub and Mayor Eva will get married?" Molly asked.

"Too early to say," I said, uncomfortable talking about the very proper mayor, but not enough to keep my mouth shut.

"My guess is she's making Dub pay for the grief he caused through the years."

"I don't know what she sees in him," Tammy said. "She could do so much better." She caught herself. "That's probably what people say about Walt marrying me."

7

Dot Plunkett reports her new knee works fine, but she wishes the doctor had replaced the one that hurt. She said after a discussion with her son from Nebraska the doctor agreed to do the other one for free.

—The Green News-Item

My father-in-law had raised the Chicken of the Future when he was in the eighth grade.

This accomplishment brought him only slightly less pride than his three fine sons.

Therefore, he thought Chris and I needed chickens to round out our lives.

"You can learn a lot from watching chickens," he said during one of our Saturday family breakfasts. "They'll calm you down, add personality to your homestead."

"Dad, we moved a Craig family home to the place where my bride's house blew away in a tornado on our wedding day. By most people's standards, that's plenty of personality for any homestead." Chris buttered one of his mother's gargantuan homemade biscuits while he spoke, his voice firm. He shot me a don't-fall-for-this look. "Thanks for the offer, though."

Nearly everyone in Green had an idea about what we should do with our house and yard, and most people knew I would do almost anything Hugh Craig said. He and Estelle had welcomed me into the family as though I were one of their own.

Hugh had taught me more about North Louisiana plants and animals than many natives knew. He often stopped by the house to visit and would jump into any project, with a vision for what our yard should look like.

"Let's hear what Lois has to say before you put the hiatus on the chickens, Son," Hugh said. "She might like to have a few guineas to raise a racket if anyone comes around. They're the best watchdogs around."

I threw Chris a look this time, trying not to smile. Hugh pulled words out of thin air and sometimes came close but just missed on their meaning. At least if we were talking about fowl, we weren't talking about the school closing, which hung over the family like a damp blanket on a hot Louisiana day.

"You have to help us out with the dogs as it is, Mr. Hugh," I said, "and we aren't going to be finished with the house for months. I'm not sure we're ready to take on another responsibility."

"Another reason you need chickens. They'll make you feel settled."

Chris sighed and pushed his chair back. "I've got to go to basketball practice."

"Chicken," I said when he leaned over to kiss me goodbye.

"Draw the line at goats or rabbits," he said in a fake whisper. "He received ribbons at the Bouef Parish Fair for those, too."

Estelle smiled as Chris gave her a hug, and she was still smiling while she washed and I dried the dishes. "If I'd known how happy you were going to make our family, I would have insisted Chris drag you over here sooner."

My sisters-in-law often chipped in and visited while we cleaned, but today they had headed out on errands, and I was glad. I loved the one-on-one chats with my mother-in-law.

"If I'd known how happy you all were going to make me, I'd have come sooner."

———⚇⚇⚇———

Rose woke us up before daylight the middle of the next week. Antique mall emergencies were rare, and I couldn't think what she might be calling about.

"Rise and shine," she said as I fumbled with the receiver and tried to figure out what time it was. "We have a package for you at the post office."

"Great. Leave it on the kitchen table like you always do. Goodbye."

"I don't think you want this on your kitchen table," she said.

"How about bringing it to your shop after work?" I asked.

"Not a chance."

The oversized clock radio, another hand-me-down after the tornado, said it was five minutes after six.

"You win, Rose. What kind of package do we have that requires the mail carrier calling in the middle of the night?"

"I could have called at five-thirty when I started sorting the mail," she said. "I think it's poultry."

"Rose, did you say 'poultry?'"

"Peep, peep," she said. "Can you or Chris pick this up before I head out on my route?"

Promising her we would pick up the box within the hour, I rolled over and nudged Chris. "You can quit pretending you're asleep. You might as well go ahead and call your father."

———⚬⚭⚬———

I was still in my warm fleece robe when Hugh pulled up. I watched from the door as he removed the box from the front seat of his spotless pickup truck.

Holly Beth dashed out to greet him, followed more slowly by Chris, who was pulling on his windbreaker to leave for work.

"They got here in a hurry," the elder Craig said. "I haven't even started on a coop for them. But we have plenty of time. They'll need to stay in that box while it's cold."

"I suppose you're referring to the chickens we agreed we didn't want," Chris said, holding the side door open and patting the clothes dryer. "Set them here until you're ready to leave."

"You'll get a kick out of them," Hugh said. "Let's at least open them up and give them a little air and water. We'll have to keep them away from the dogs, though."

"That'll be easy," his son said. "We only have four that we have no control over." To prove my point, he tried to put Holly in her crate while she ran around the room with a chew toy in her mouth.

I finally corralled her, spoke to her firmly the way the dog-training book advised and locked her up, ignoring her annoyed barks.

"I like that girl of yours, Son." Hugh smiled at me, looking a lot more chipper than I felt. "She has spunk."

"Well, you and Ms. Spunk have fun with the chickens. I've got a parent-teacher conference and need to ride herd on a few dozen kids." Chris gave me a goodbye kiss. "Good luck with the chicken whisperer."

"You're leaving me with your father and a box of chickens and an irritated dog?"

JUDY CHRISTIE

"'Fraid so." He kissed me again, a teasing light in his eyes. "I can't wait to hear how this turns out, but I'm putting my money on you."

A dozen and a half chicks chirped loudly when Hugh pried the top off of the box. "My goodness," my father-in-law said. "This order's mixed up. I only asked for ten."

"You ordered us ten chickens?" The question was not asked in my nicest tone.

Hugh sounded slightly put out. "You need variety to decide which kind you like best. Then we can order more of that type."

"This is a thoughtful idea, but we don't have time to fool with chickens." I needed to get to work and didn't want to hurt his feelings. I shouldn't have worried, though, because he acted like he hadn't heard me and put one of the tiny balls of fluff in my hand. The little heart beat rapidly, and the chick shivered until I cupped it gently.

"Do you have any newspapers?" Hugh asked, and then laughed. "Silly question."

While he lined the box with several back issues of my precious *News-Item*, I inspected the shipping slip. "They sent a dozen as filler," I said. "These extra little guys are like packing peanuts."

Hugh filled one of my favorite bowls with water, a piece of pottery I'd picked up at Rose's antique store the week before, and set it in the box. "I hope the extras aren't all roosters," he said. "That'll cause quite a racket."

─────

By the time Chris and I got home from work, the chicks were huddled under a lamp I had never seen before, the box still wedged on top of the dryer, with a bag of chicken feed on the washer.

"Will come by tomorrow to start on the pen," Hugh had scrawled on a paper towel.

"I guess we're raising chickens." I picked one up and handed it to Chris.

"I was counting on you to tell him you'd visit them on weekends in his yard," my husband said, but I could tell the chick had softened his irritation. I petted another one, hoping it wouldn't poop on my hand.

"You thought they'd put me in a fowl mood, didn't you?" Chris said and placed the chick back in the box. "I'm sure my father crowed all the way home."

I stood on my tiptoes to give Chris a hearty kiss, still laughing at his bad jokes.

"I'll fix up a place for them in the travel trailer for now," he said. "Maybe we can figure something out."

"Didn't Rick mention a carpenter staying in the camper?" I asked. "There's so much going on that I can't quite recall, but it seems like someone needed it after Joe Sepulvado turned it down."

Chris picked up the box of chicks. "Rick never followed up on that, so I assumed it didn't work out."

"If someone does move into the camper, I hope they don't mind sharing with chicks."

"Something tells me these aren't the kind of chicks they'd be interested in living with," Chris said.

"Supper will be ready in fifteen minutes," I said. "No poultry on the menu."

He grinned and walked outside.

Chris's grin had turned to a frown when he returned, his cheeks red from the cold. He washed his hands at the sink and put ice in our tea glasses.

"Things are a little off in the camper," Chris said. "There's a toothbrush, that kind of thing, but nobody's around. I wonder if Rick assigned a carpenter to stay there and forgot to tell us?"

"You don't think those meth dealers came back, do you?" I got up and latched the back door.

"They don't strike me as dental floss kind of guys," Chris said. "It's probably one of the construction crew."

"Do you think we should call the sheriff?"

Standing at the used stove, Chris dished our food onto donated plates, both chipped. He had the perplexed look he wore when he was trying to figure out an answer to a construction problem.

"I think everything's OK. They've locked up a half dozen of the meth dealers, and no one would have anything to gain by poking around here after six months."

"The dogs would let us know if anyone were outside," I said.

"Or our two guinea chicks would."

Dressing for work the next morning, I heard Chris talking in the kitchen and saw the contractor's truck at the side of the driveway, leaving room for us to pull in and out.

"You're getting an early start," I said, barging into the kitchen with a smile. "I hope Chris offered you a cup of . . ." My voice trailed off. There, sitting next to our builder, was one of the first people who had tried to hurt me in Green.

Lee Roy Hicks wore workman's coveralls and an orange stocking cap, his blond hair barely showing under the hat.

I stopped so suddenly that Holly Beth, right on my heels, ran into me and barked.

Scooping her into my arms, I moved close to Chris.

"I thought he was still in jail." I hated the way my heart pounded, here in my own kitchen, beating harder than the little chick's had yesterday when I picked it up.

Lee Roy looked as shocked to see me as I was to see him. His face paled, and sweat popped out on his temples, below the cap.

"In jail?" Chris looked puzzled and put his arm around me. "Lois, Rick wanted to introduce us to Lee here. He's come on board with the building company and will be staying out here to keep an eye on things when we're not around."

The comfort of Chris's embrace calmed me, and I moved closer. "That man isn't coming within ten feet of this house. Don't you recognize him?"

"Have we met before?" Chris was confused. Lee Roy looked as though he wished he could evaporate into thin air, and Rick seemed to think I had lost my mind.

My former advertising manager stood, pulled the stocking cap off and held out his hand. Chris extended his right hand, still holding me close, and then it dawned on him who the man was and he froze.

A rare angry look came to my husband's eyes, and both men awkwardly dropped their hands.

"You have a lot of nerve showing up here," Chris said.

He shielded me with his body. Holly, annoyed to be wedged between us, wiggled down and ran first to Rick and then to Lee Roy, sniffing their boots.

"I don't want to cause any trouble," Lee Roy said. He turned to his boss. "When you said I'd be helping on the Craig place,

I didn't make the connection with Lois Barker. I'd better get going."

He turned for the door, Holly Beth playing around his feet. He bent to pet her as he reached for the doorknob. "You're a cute little thing," he said, and stepped out.

Rick looked as though someone had put his thoughts into a blender. Every one of them, from confusion to dismay, ran across his face.

"I'm sorry, Lois. So much has changed in Green since I lived here before. I never even considered you knew Lee. I had no idea you'd had problems with him before."

"Lee? That man's name is Lee Roy."

"He goes by Lee now," the builder said. "I hired him through a program to give first-time offenders a second chance. As you evidently know, he had trouble with the law and is trying to make a fresh start."

I exhaled. "And that fresh start happens to be at my house? The woman he stole from and attacked in a parking lot?"

"I've made a terrible mistake. I'm sorry." Rick looked us both in the face. "I originally had him doing a job on the lake but needed him over here. You two are quick to help people out, so I figured you wouldn't mind that he had a record."

"When that record involves my wife, I mind a lot," Chris said.

"This is the first time I've participated in this program," Rick said. "I'll know better next time."

The young builder was so mortified that I felt sorry for him, but my heart still pounded hard at the sight of Lee Roy in our kitchen. I wouldn't have been more surprised if I'd walked in and seen the black bear that got in the newspaper Dumpster year before last.

Holly whined and scratched at the back door. "Lois, if you'll let her out, Rick and I will clear this up." Chris squeezed my hand.

"It was an honest mistake," Rick said.

"Yours or Lee Roy's?" I asked, picking up Holly's leash.

"Assigning him to your project. I can't speak to his crime, but he told me he had done wrong and was trying to put his life back in order."

"Well, he can put it back in order someplace else." I grabbed my jacket, jerked open the door and stalked out, pulling Holly along.

My pulse raced, and I pictured Lee Roy grabbing me in the dark parking lot at the *Item*. Focusing on my little dog, I drew deep breaths. "Lord, quieten my heart," I prayed, words I had learned from Jean in a sermon after the tornado. "Please."

Seeming unaware of my distress, Holly sniffed around the yard in her usual routine, ran to her favorite tree, peed, and then tugged me toward the travel trailer.

"The chickens are off limits," I said and tried to direct her back to the house. "Come on. We're going to be late for work." *Had I really said that to a dog?*

The three other dogs raced up and down the fence, trying to get our attention. Already calmer, I pulled the sandwich bag of treats out of my pocket and gave each a dog biscuit and a kind word. "You be good today. Don't try to get out of the fence. You're the best dogs ever," I said, and they whined and seemed almost to smile at me.

OK, maybe I was turning into a dog person, and Lee Roy couldn't hurt me anymore.

Using the breathing exercises I vaguely remembered from a yoga class in Dayton, I felt the tension begin to dissolve.

I turned around, relaxed and ready to face the day, and my heart jumped into my throat. I had not noticed Lee Roy sitting on the steps of the small trailer, his head in his hands. Even though it was a cold morning, he had not put the cap back on and had his fingers woven through his hair.

Holly saw him about the same time I did and pulled me toward him, yelping like she had spotted a long-lost friend. Surprised, I loosened my grip on the leash, and she pulled away and ran right to him. I followed hesitantly.

He looked up at the dog with what might have almost seemed like delight if it hadn't been on the face of such a rotten man, and scooped Holly into his lap. He scratched her under her neck, exactly as she preferred, and talked softly to her. As I approached, he set her on the ground and reached out to hand me her leash.

"What do you think you're doing?" I asked, backing away while trying to scoop Holly Beth up. "We told you to get off our property."

"I'm sorry." Lee Roy looked embarrassed and touched his watch. "I'm waiting for a ride. The rest of the crew should be here any minute, and I'll ask one of them to take me back to town."

"That's a far cry from that fancy gold watch you used to wear," I said, nodding at the inexpensive watch with a plain face and black band.

"Everything in my life is a far cry from what it used to be," he said. "I want to apologize again. I hope you've been getting the restitution payments."

"Iris Jo and Linda handle those," I said. "I don't want anything to do with you."

"That's understandable." He seemed to shrink into the insulated coveralls. "I wouldn't want to have anything to do with me either."

He gestured toward the building site. "I'm sorry about your house blowing away, but I like what you and Chris are doing. The guys are going to make this into a fine place to live."

"Rick does great work," I said, forgetting for a split second who I was talking to. "He's helping us make the best of a bad situation."

"He's good about that," Lee Roy said, petting Holly once more. The contact with the dog changed his entire demeanor. "I hope I don't get fired over this."

"That's between you and Rick." I looked over my shoulder, hoping Chris might wonder why I was taking so long and rescue me from this conversation.

"I didn't come here to cause any trouble," he said. "I swear to you I had no idea this was your place, that you and Chris had gotten married. That must have happened while I was . . . away." He coughed. "While I was in jail."

"Our wedding was almost a year ago."

"Congratulations. The Craigs are good people. Mr. Hugh visited me while I was in jail."

"Hugh Craig?"

"He came with a group from a church downtown," Lee Roy said. "It meant a lot to me when he sought me out, talked about where I had gone wrong. He was the first one to start calling me Lee. He said a new name might help with my new start."

While I was still trying to process that news, the side door of the house opened, and Rick stepped out, Chris right behind. Chris looked around the yard until he spotted me, and his eyes narrowed when he saw Lee Roy.

"Hicks, why are you still here? Lois, are you OK?" Chris shouted, his tone so alarmed that the three bigger dogs started growling and barking. My husband rushed to my side, standing between me and the man.

"Everything's good," I said. "He needs a ride to town. Can you drop him on your way to school?"

That question startled my husband, and Rick jumped in. "I'll take him. Wait in the truck, until I clear things up with these folks."

Lee Roy nodded at his boss and headed for the road. Holly chased after him before I could stop her, and he petted her again and then pointed to us. I couldn't hear what he said to her, but she trotted back our way.

"I should never have gotten mixed up in that work-release program in the first place," Rick said. "I don't know what I was thinking."

"You were trying to do the right thing," Chris said, "to help someone out."

"He's been a model employee for the past three months," Rick said. "I never expected a problem like this."

I looked out at the road, at Lee Roy sitting in the truck, his head once more in his hands, and thought about what he'd said about Hugh's visit and about Jean's words. *If one of us falls down . . .*

"You're not going to fire him, are you?" I wasn't sure if the question surprised me or Chris more.

"Of course I'm going to fire him. This is how I earn my living. I can't take chances with that. I won't make this mistake again."

"Do you know part of each of his paychecks goes to the *News-Item*?" I asked.

Rick shook his head. "That comes through the parish. We hold it out for him, and they send it."

"If you fire him, how will he pay me back?" I asked.

Chris began shaking his head. "Lois, that man attacked you. No telling what he would have done if Rose hadn't called the police that night in the parking lot."

"He scared me, but he didn't hurt me. He did wrong, and I don't like him." I rubbed Chris's jacket sleeve. "But if Rick fires him, nobody will hire him. Then I won't get any of the money back."

"The money's not a big deal," Chris said. "I'm not going to take a chance that he's going to hurt you. He's probably holding a grudge against you for sending him to jail in the first place."

I threw my eyes toward the truck. "That man doesn't look like he has the energy to hold a grudge."

"Lois, whatever you're thinking, the answer is no." Chris kicked at a rock.

Rick's eyes went back and forth as we spoke, as though watching a tennis match.

"We're not taking a chance." I grabbed Chris by the hand. "We're offering a chance."

Chris, who did more for others than anyone I had ever met, would have a hard time with that line of thinking.

"We'll find someone else who needs help," he said. "There's a list a mile long on Pastor Jean's desk."

"Why look at a list when we're staring at someone right now?" I said.

Chris shook his head again. "Lois, I've got to go to work. I've got hall duty this morning, and Priscilla watches the faculty like a hawk."

"Could we compromise?" I asked.

"You mean ask Rick to put him on another job site?" he asked.

"I mean ask Rick to keep a closer eye on him. Since a big part of his check goes to the newspaper, it'll be like free work on the house."

"You're trying to make up for Joe Sepulvado getting arrested by mistake last year, aren't you? You feel guilty, and you want to make it up by helping this guy."

"I feel a little guilty," I said. "But Lee Roy says your dad visited him in jail. Maybe we need to help, too."

"You don't owe Lee Roy Hicks one thing."

"Maybe I owe myself something," I said and looked at Rick, who was scuffing his boot in the dirt in the driveway, as though he'd rather be almost anywhere else. "Marrying you has made me a nicer person."

Chris cleared his throat, and I realized I'd embarrassed him in front of the builder. "You were plenty nice before."

"So do I fire him or not?" Rick asked quietly. Two pickups carrying members of his crew drove up. "We're burning daylight here."

"Keep a close eye on him," Chris said. "I trust your judgment."

I hugged my husband.

Chris reached out to shake Rick's hand. "I look forward to the day you get married, man. It'll rock your world."

8

*Alan Bottoms on Railroad Crossing Road has a
two-headed turtle to give away. His father, who lives
on Caddo Lake, found it under the house last week, only
a few days after he discovered an albino rattlesnake
behind his firewood. "Daddy doesn't move as fast as
he used to, so that rattler got away before he could hit
it with the hoe," Alan said. "But that turtle is
free for the taking."*

—The Green News-Item

Anthony dribbled the ball down court at his usual quick pace, looking around for someone to take a pass. Chris stood on the sidelines, motioning for him to keep going.

As the boy turned his head, a guard from the visiting team slammed into him. The ball flew out of bounds, Anthony hit the floor, and the Green crowd jumped to its feet, demanding a foul.

The raucous shouts grew silent when Anthony didn't bounce up.

An eerie hush came over the Rabbits gym, while Chris and a volunteer assistant rushed out onto the court, joined by referees.

The teen was sprawled on the floor, his eyes closed. He didn't move.

"Oh, no," Kevin said. Her tone left no doubt that she had noticed something I hadn't. "Will you watch Asa while I help?"

JUDY CHRISTIE

She had already begun to push her way through the crowd, a path opening for her.

I tried to distract her child, who began to cry as Kevin disappeared into the rows of people. He quieted when Kevin reappeared next to Anthony. She knelt on the floor next to Chris and spoke into Anthony's ear, but he didn't move, nor did his eyes open.

Molly, standing on the edge of the court, covered her face with her hands. Tammy set her camera down and put her arm around the girl. The assistant coach rushed to the outdated black phone hanging on the wall at the end of the gym and dialed three numbers.

———

The emergency room at the hospital overflowed with students, parents, and Anthony's mother, little sister, and baby brother. Nearly two hours had passed since the ambulance had arrived, and early reports were grim.

An orthopedic surgeon rushed in and conferred with Kevin near the cubicle where EMTs had rolled Anthony, but we couldn't hear what was being said.

Chris paced in front of the row of chairs where I sat, his mouth a tight line. Molly cried quietly, comforted by Iris Jo, Stan, and a steady stream of players and other students. The room had taken on the smell of a sweaty locker room, the athletes still in uniform.

My cell phone vibrated, and I saw it was Katy calling. I stepped outside, hoping for better reception. The cold air was a sharp contrast to the overheated room, and the ambulance was parked nearby, two EMTs waiting in the front seat, radio audible through the closed windows.

"Katy?" I said. "Can you hear me?"

96

"Lois, what's going on? I got a garbled message from Molly. Did someone get hurt?"

"It's Anthony. He was injured at the game tonight. They don't know how bad yet."

"Where's Molly?"

"We're all at the hospital. She's inside with Anthony's mother."

"I wish I was there," Katy said, tears evident in her voice. "I don't know what to do."

"All we can do is wait and pray," I said. "I'll text you as soon as we hear anything. Try to get some sleep."

"Tell Molly I love her."

As the automatic doors slid open to let me back inside, the entire crowd in the ER began to move.

I rushed up to Chris. "What's happening? Where's everyone going?"

"They're moving Anthony to intensive care and calling a neurosurgeon in Shreveport. It doesn't look good, and it's my fault. I distracted him."

⚬⚬⚬

Through the night the crowd dwindled, sent home by Kevin, who put on a lab coat and transformed from a basketball fan to a somber physician.

"Go home and rest," she said to the students, who had jumped to their feet when she entered the room. "When Anthony regains consciousness, he'll need you more."

Marcus and Pearl, Asa's grandparents, had taken Kevin's son home from the game, and Iris Jo and Stan insisted on keeping Anthony's eight-year-old sister and toddler brother, who had fallen asleep on the floor.

97

"Pastor Jean will help tomorrow," Iris said to Anthony's mother, Anita. "Let us do this for you."

Anita was a few years younger than I but had the look of a woman who had seen more than her share of grief. She wore her nursing-home aide uniform, her name tag pinned to the blue top. The words "How may I help you?" were printed on the tag.

The woman, whom I had met a year ago under less-than-ideal circumstances, started to protest and then gave in, tears running down her cheeks. She hugged and kissed the children, the toddler never waking. "Mama loves you," she said. "You be good for Miss Iris Jo."

"Yes, ma'am." The little girl nodded as though she understood the seriousness of the situation. As Iris helped her put on her coat, she looked over at me. "I still have that teddy bear you gave me. It's real cute."

"She sleeps with it every night," Anita said as she watched her daughter walk out holding Iris Jo's hand. "I can never thank you enough for bringing that food and getting us out of that horrible place."

"Chris did most of that," I said with a smile. "He's good at things like that."

"But you and that woman," she nodded at Tammy, "were the ones who got us away from my awful boyfriend. Vince was a bad man. Thanks to you he's been sent away."

I didn't like to think about the meth dealer who had attacked me and Tammy. I certainly didn't want Chris to hear us talking about it. He and Walt still had not forgiven us for our encounter with Vince, who was in jail for selling drugs.

"Why don't you try to get some sleep in one of those chairs, Anita? I'll turn the lights down." I embraced her, not at all awkwardly as I might once have, but fiercely, wishing I could protect her from the pain of bad choices, an abusive boyfriend, and now this terrible accident.

"Show me how to help" was my unspoken plea.

———◦∞∞◦———

Kevin tried to talk Molly into leaving, but she refused. She sat down next to Anita and took the woman's hand. Chris kept pacing, occasionally sitting down next to me, only to stand up within seconds.

"You need to go home, Lois," he said quietly when I fished around in a cabinet for coffee cups. "There's no point in staying all night."

"Are you staying?"

"I have to," he said.

"Then I'm staying." I put my arms around him and felt a shudder run through his body. "We'll get through this together."

———◦∞∞◦———

While the downstairs area sweltered, the ICU waiting room was frigid, and I walked to the nursing station to ask for blankets for Molly and Anita. Behind the counter, Kevin sat with a chart in her lap, her eyes closed.

She looked up as I got close.

"Resting?" I asked.

She shook her head. "Praying."

"How bad is it?"

She looked over my shoulder to make sure no one was within earshot. "I tell you this because you and Chris have been like family to Anthony."

I nodded. "I won't say anything to anyone but Chris."

"Preliminary tests don't show spine damage, but we're concerned about a head injury."

I could feel the color draining from my face. "What do we do now?"

"Continue to monitor him," she said, "and hope he opens his eyes soon. When he stabilizes, we'll have to move him to Shreveport. We don't have the expertise or equipment here to handle this long-term."

"Long-term?"

"Lois, it's too soon to know for sure, but there's a possibility that Anthony may never recover from this."

The next few days were a blur of hard chairs, nerve-wracking phone calls, and heartbreaking moments with Molly, who tried to manage work, school, and driving to the hospital in Shreveport, where Anthony had been transported by helicopter. He had regained consciousness the morning after the accident but still had not moved his legs.

Alicia and Adam, Anthony's little sister and brother, stayed with Iris Jo and Stan, who took them to school and day care respectively and made it to work, never complaining.

"It's kind of nice, actually," Iris said at her desk late in the week. "I haven't had a child in the house in a long time, and Stan never had children. It's been fun watching him with them."

Along with a cartoon sticker on her shirt, she had a sparkle in her eye, similar to the one the day she had eloped with Stan, only six of us watching Pastor Jean perform the service. Since her chemo, her hair was short and curlier.

"Anita told me yesterday at the hospital that she didn't know what she'd do without you two. As far as I can tell, she doesn't have any family support."

"We're her family now," Iris said. "When Matt died, everyone stepped up for me, and that's what I want to do for Anita and Anthony."

Iris Jo's teenage son, Matt, had been killed in a car wreck more than four years earlier. He'd been Katy's boyfriend. A quiet, calm woman, Iris shone with faith and kindness.

"Watching Anita and Molly, I can't help but think about what you and Katy went through when Matt died," I said. "I'm sure it's on Molly's mind, too."

"Somehow it will work out," she said, the words so often spoken in this community.

They were also the words I used with Chris on Saturday morning when we headed for Shreveport after breakfast with his parents. Usually he reminded me how things turn out for the best. I wanted to be there for him so badly that it scared me, to help him feel better as he had done so many times for me, to remind him of what a good man he was.

"I can't see how this can ever be OK," he said. "That boy can't walk. I keep seeing him fall over and over, wondering what I could have done differently."

"It was an accident," I said. "Everyone agrees he fell at the wrong angle because of a hard hit."

"I shouldn't have motioned to him. Or I could have taught him how to take a shove like that better," Chris said. "Or made sure the floor wasn't so slick."

"You're a wonderful coach and a good friend to your players. You were there for Anthony when his family was hungry, and you've been there since this happened—and with his classmates, with the school situation on top of the accident."

"It's hard to feel very positive right now."

"I know," I said. "But lots of people are willing to help."

With near-constant visitors and a level of high-school unruliness, the Shreveport hospital had set up a special waiting area for Anthony's friends and family, a steady stream of Green residents in and out. Nearly a dozen people were already on hand when we arrived, and everyone's look brightened when Chris entered the room.

"He's doing better this morning, Coach," one of the players said. "His mom said he was asking to see you."

When Anita came to get Chris, he jumped to his feet, moving faster than he had since right after the injury. "They won't let anyone stay for long," she said, almost apologetically, "but he wants to talk to you."

As they walked away, I gave thanks again for my husband and asked God to soothe his heart.

A small disturbance sounded outside the visitor's lounge, and my heart leapt into my throat. All eyes turned to the door, distress on many faces.

Katy swept in, a big grin on her face, and the room let out an audible sigh of relief. "Lois," the girl squealed. "I hoped you'd be here."

Molly was on her heels, subdued but smiling. "She drove in after classes yesterday. Wasn't that sweet?"

My mind sorted the surprised delight of seeing Katy, her new bright red hairstyle and the fact she had driven from the University of Georgia on a Friday night. "With who?" I asked.

"All by my lonesome, me and my tunes. My new car is fantastic." The car, a snappy little red number, had been a high-school graduation gift from her mother and her stepfather, the now-controversial superintendent of schools in Bouef Parish. I wasn't sure if James had agreed to the car because of how proud he was of Katy or how thankful he was that he'd lived through her high-school days.

"She's staying till Monday," Molly said. "Isn't it good to have her home?"

"Don't you have class?" I once more sounded sharper than intended.

"I'm skipping. Those freshman classes are so big, they'll never notice, and I've got an 'A' average in all my classes."

Turning to greet former classmates, she squealed again, and Molly smiled at me and shook her head, looking older than her eighteen years. "She never changes, does she?"

I put my arm around her. "How are you holding up?"

"Pretty good." She put her head on my shoulder. "It's been a hard week, but I know it'll get better. It helps having Katy home."

When Chris returned from the ICU, his eyes looked red. He greeted Katy and Molly, looking over their heads at me with a sad expression.

"How's he doing this morning, Coach?" Molly asked. "Ready to play basketball?"

"Just about." His jovial tone didn't match the look in his eyes. "He's looking forward to getting back on the court."

The room emptied around noon, leaving Chris and me alone with Walt and Tammy, who had arrived in time for an exuberant reunion with Katy. Walt wore his standard khakis and blue oxford shirt and chatted comfortably with a variety of acquaintances in the room.

Tammy, nearly fifteen years his junior, wore an expensive pair of jeans and a designer blouse I had seen at Eva's department store. The clothes were a contrast to the inexpensive outfits she had worn before marrying the attorney. She looked about the same age as Katy and Molly.

"Walt surprised me with a gift certificate for our wedding anniversary," she said when I complimented her on the outfit.

"I told him I didn't need another new outfit. He's given me so many pretty clothes already."

"But you haven't had your anniversary yet. You've only been married since September."

"Our four-month anniversary." She grinned. "He gets me a gift every month."

I looked over at the bookish man, chatting with my athletic husband, and smiled. "We hit the jackpot, didn't we?"

"It's way more than I deserve." She fingered her engagement ring.

Over lunch at a nearby Italian restaurant, the four of us discussed what the future might hold for Anthony.

"He told me they're not sure what's wrong with him." Chris paused. "But they can't guarantee he won't be in a wheelchair the rest of his life."

The olive mix on the salad hung in my throat, and I coughed. Tammy gasped.

"That's a lot for anyone to handle, especially a teenager," Walt said. "He's fortunate to have you as his friend."

"I hope I can be half as strong as he is," Chris replied. "He had to grow up way too early, and he's giving this everything he's got."

―――――

After more than a week in the ICU, Anthony was moved to a room. Molly had class, and Chris had a faculty meeting, and I was happy that my name was on today's visitation roster. The Booster Club had set up an elaborate plan for visits, meals, and general help for Anita, and I always got more from the encounters than I gave.

Anthony's bed was empty when I arrived, though, and my hand flew to my mouth.

"May I help you, ma'am?" I turned to see a young woman in green scrubs.

"Anthony Cox?" I was afraid even to say his name.

"He's in physical therapy," the woman said, and air filled my lungs again. "He should be back anytime. His mother went to the cafeteria."

Debating whether to wait in the room or search for Anita, I looked at the many cards displayed on the window ledge. One was hand-drawn with a portrait that bore a striking resemblance to the player. He was holding the hand of a little girl. "To my big brother," it said in crayon.

I opened it, and read the childish scrawl. "Get well soon. Love, Alicia." I sniffed and held the card against my body.

"She thinks Anthony hung the moon," Anita said behind me. I jumped and dropped the card, embarrassed at reading the messages and clutching the card.

"He's heard from everyone, even the governor. He got the balloons from the newspaper staff this morning," she said, pointing to a gigantic assortment with ribbons of every color. "He especially liked the one shaped like a basketball."

"That was Tammy's idea."

I patted the one chair in the room, and Anita sank into it, as though her body was suddenly too heavy for her legs. I leaned back against the bed. The room was silent except for medical machines clicking every now and then, a medicinal smell in the air.

"Is Anthony better today?" I asked finally.

She slowly shook her head. "He still can't walk, but they can't find anything wrong with him."

"They'll figure it out. Chris says these are the best orthopedic doctors in the South. He has seen them work with other teams, and they go the extra mile for their patients."

"Coach has been so good to us." Anita pleated the sheet with her fingers. "After all I put you through, I don't deserve it. I am so sorry."

"You have nothing to apologize for. Vince was no match for Tammy and her baseball bat." I tried to laugh, but the memory of the encounter was too painful, and it sounded like I was choking.

"It's not only that," she said. "I was rude to you when you tried to help."

"That's in the past." I wished Chris were here. He was much better at sensitive situations than I was.

"I was ashamed to take that food," she said. "That's not an excuse, but I knew I had let my kids down. What kind of a mother does something like that?"

"You're a good mother. Your children adore you."

"I wasn't there when Anthony got hurt." Her voice was barely above a whisper. "I missed his game to work an extra shift. If I had been there . . ."

"You've been to lots of his games. He understands you have to work."

She broke down, apologizing between sobs. "I haven't cried all week, but you're so easy to talk to."

I rubbed Anita's arm, remembering for a moment how my mother had soothed me when I cried as a child. "I'm scared, Miss Lois. My boy may never be able to walk again, and the treatment costs so much money. I've missed nearly two weeks of work already, and my boss is running out of patience."

"We'll figure something out. Green always steps up." I paused. "Tell me how I can help you."

As word of Anthony's imminent return home spread, members of local churches rushed over to build a wheelchair ramp at the family's tiny mobile home.

Kevin and her partner donated an array of medical supplies, and students and teachers chipped in to buy the athlete his own television with headphones. The Green cheerleaders made a "Welcome home" banner and lined the yard with streamers.

Iris showed up with a large box of new toys for Alicia and Adam. "We didn't want them to feel left out. We hope Anita will let us keep them again."

"They deserve good things in their lives," Stan said, the gruff tone showing emotions he tried to hide.

He leaned down and hugged the two children as they ran up and grabbed him around his knees, an expression on his face I had never seen before, the delight and love a father shows when he sees his children after a long absence.

Chris and I gathered with a small crowd to welcome Anthony as he arrived in a medical transport van. Molly pushed him from the driveway to the house, Alicia running out to sit in his lap.

My husband reached over and gave my hand a squeeze as the wheelchair rolled out of sight. "I hate to leave," he said, sounding like he had a frog in his throat, "but we have a game tonight."

9

Madeline Howell wants everyone to quit worrying about closing the school and consider a new dress code. "With seven children —two in elementary, three in junior high and a set of twins in high school—uniforms would make sorting laundry much easier," she said at our annual block party.

—The Green News-Item

Cars lined the shoulders of the road and were parked on the school lawn.

"Looks like we got us a crowd for the meeting," my mother-in-law said, climbing out of her truck as I walked by. "Where's my son?"

"I haven't seen him since he left for school this morning." I gave each of Chris's parents a short hug. "Between his visiting Anthony, coaching, teaching, and trying to keep his coworkers from killing the new principal, I haven't seen much of him these past couple of weeks."

"This was a good idea your newspaper had, bringing the community together to talk about this mess," Hugh said. "Who ever heard of such a thing? A town like Green isn't much of a town without its school."

As we crossed the driveway where school buses dropped students each morning, a big black Mercedes with Texas plates whipped in and wedged its way between two SUVs, blocking the sidewalk.

"Well, my goodness," Estelle said, stepping around the car.

"Sorry," Marcus Hillburn said, climbing from the vehicle and pulling a sports coat from a hanger in the back. "I came from Austin, and I'm running late."

"He doesn't sound sorry at all, if you ask me," Estelle whispered loudly as he barreled past a cluster of parents and young children.

"He's sorry, all right," my father-in-law said.

"Now, Hugh," Estelle replied.

The gym was three-quarters full when we entered, and a steady stream of people filed in behind us, jockeying for seats. A line of metal folding chairs sat under one of the goals, behind a lectern made in a wood-shop class and pulled out for special occasions.

My eyes scanned the court, looking for Chris, who saw me first. He waved and started toward us, stopping to speak to Anthony, who wheeled himself in with the skill of a pro. Chris helped an elderly woman navigate the bleachers, directed a preschooler to her mother, and picked up two pieces of trash from the shiny floor, all while working his way to us.

"Chris loves this school," his mother said, stepping forward to greet him. "You've got this gym shining, Son."

"You sure do." I took my turn—and my time—hugging him. "Long day?"

He sighed and nodded, and the fatigue showed in his eyes. "I hope you're ready for fireworks tonight. I've never seen people so worked up."

As we chatted, the noise level in the room grew, everyone getting caught up with neighbors and expressing opinions on closing the school.

"I wouldn't want to be in the superintendent's shoes tonight," Hugh said.

I agreed. "I'm glad I'm not moderating this one. All I have to do is say 'welcome' and turn it over to that crew." I nodded toward the end where Katy's father, James, stood with Priscilla Robinson, Marcus, the mayor, and two school board members.

"Sure feels different from game nights, doesn't it?" Chris said.

I had a hard time quieting the crowd to make opening remarks and was happy to hand the microphone, with its perpetual hum, to the principal.

"We are delighted that so many of you have turned out this evening," Priscilla said. "We are to here to clear up rumors that have been flying and falsehoods that the media have been spreading."

I glanced across at Chris and other teachers, and my husband caught my eye and gave a small smile.

"Oh, brother," Tammy said, shoving her way onto the bleacher next to me and placing her camera on the floor. "This should be fun."

"We are all here tonight for one reason—because we want to do what's best for the children. With that in mind, I suggest that everyone be respectful and polite," the administrator continued. She looked like a model in a women's magazine in a skirt and matching jacket. My only consolation was that she had to be sweltering in the hot gym.

Katy's father was not nearly as polished a speaker, fumbling with his notes as he pulled a pair of reading glasses out of his jacket pocket. "This talk of consolidation hurts me more than it hurts you," he said.

"I doubt it," a young father wearing a power company uniform yelled.

"If it hurts you so much, don't do it," a woman said loudly.

The crowd applauded, and Priscilla Robinson jumped up from her chair and elbowed James out of the way.

"Ladies and gentlemen," she said, "if we cannot conduct ourselves with decorum this evening, we will shut this meeting down immediately."

"Don't scold us like we're in kindergarten," a middle-aged woman hollered.

Priscilla jutted her chin out and squinted her eyes, but James spoke to her and reclaimed control of the public address system. He laid his notes down, took off his sport coat, detached the microphone from its stand, and walked onto the court, the cord trailing. The crowd noise went from a dull roar to a restless murmur.

"I'm a Green High School graduate," he said. "So are my wife and stepdaughter and many members of my family. I bleed green-and-white. But we simply cannot afford to keep all of our schools open and provide quality education to our students."

"Then shut down the other ones," someone shouted.

James held up his hand for silence. "We have studied the financial situation from every angle, and we agree with the state and outside experts that we need to move Green's students elsewhere. As you know, we have asked the school board to approve this action."

The crowd did not applaud when he sat down, but it also did not boo. I was relieved. Although I didn't agree with James, I thought too much of him and his family to see him treated poorly.

Marcus had the task of explaining statistics to the crowd, which was much like trying to tell Asa why he should eat vegetables. "Quite frankly, your graduation rate is not what it needs to be. Enrollment dropped last year, and attendance percentages are down."

"You try to go to school when your house has been blown away," a local businessman shouted, and the crowd clapped again. "You weren't here for our tornado. Now you're making us suffer all over again."

Marcus crossed his arms across his chest, bumping the microphone and scowling. His face softened when Eva stood, whispered in his ear, and took the microphone. His satisfied look didn't last long.

"I think I speak for this very enthusiastic crowd when I say we're prepared to do whatever we can to save our schools," Eva said, looking at the consultant. The mayor looked even more commanding than Priscilla Robinson. "My question to you, sir, is what is the precise deadline we face?"

At first, Marcus looked like a butterfly pinned to one of the posters in the science classroom, but I could almost see the change come over him, like an actor switching from an angry character to a pleasant one.

He didn't take the mike when Eva pushed it at him, but draped an arm around her shoulder as though they were old buddies and spoke loudly. "You have until the end of this school year, ninety days from last Friday. You can do this the easy way or the hard way, but the state plans to close this school at the end of this semester."

Eva moved away from Marcus with the grace of a dancer and spoke into the microphone. "Green has never been known to take the easy way out," she said, staring directly into her ex-husband's eyes.

She dropped the microphone, which dangled with a repeated "thump," and strode to midcourt, asking the crowd to rise. "I ask you all to join with me as we rally 'round Green," she said. "We will not give up our school without a fight." Without another word, she marched right out of the gym, many in the crowd following.

⚬⚬⚬

Eva berated Marcus for jumping into Green's business—and herself for not seeing it coming.

"I can't stand that smug look on Marc's face," she said. "What makes him think he can stroll in here and turn my life—and my town—upside down again?"

She sat behind her antique Oriental desk at the department store, and I tried not to slouch in her newly refinished side chairs, handpicked on one of her trips to London. The mayor was a woman with many facets, and I was witnessing one I'd never seen.

"The state springs this on us as a fait accompli. I had my head in the sand, believing they couldn't possibly do to Green what they've done to scores of schools around the country."

"None of us paid attention to the warning signs," I said.

"Everyone was too busy getting back on their feet after the tornado," she said. "I thought I had the school board's word that they wouldn't let this happen."

"My impression is that the board didn't see it coming either." I gripped the carved arms of the chair. "They thought the state would come through with money like it always has. No one projected the cuts to be so deep."

Eva opened a file folder and thumbed through a stack of papers, finally pulling one from the group. "Our sales tax revenue is down significantly since the storm. The influx of building projects hasn't made up for the lack of spending in other areas."

"People are hurting," I said. "They can't afford to buy more than necessities."

113

"Closing the school will hurt them even more," she said. "Between the new bypass and no school, we could be facing difficult days."

Eva's personal assistant hurried into the room, a look of alarm on her face. "Mayor, that school fellow from Texas is here," she said. "He says you'll see him, even though he doesn't have an appointment."

The emotions that played across Eva's face ran the gamut from anger to surprise to an unusual look of uncertainty. "Send him in."

I started to stand, but she gave a quick shake of her head. "Don't you dare think of leaving me alone with that snake."

Marcus walked in like the chairman of the board but halted when he saw me. "I apologize for interrupting," he said. As my mother-in-law had noted the evening before, his words did not match his tone.

He wore a tailored suit and muted tie. His thick gray hair was combed in one of those styles that looked casual yet sophisticated. His shoes were so well polished that they glowed. He was a handsome man in his early sixties, with the same sort of controlled bearing that Eva usually had.

"I dare say my assistant would have been more than happy to set up an appointment," Eva said.

"My schedule is very unpredictable." He gave a smile that was probably intended to be charming but looked evil. "I meant to connect with you before that debacle of a meeting last night, but I was delayed in Austin."

The mayor raised her eyebrows and tapped her manicured nail on the telephone receiver. "Perhaps you could have picked up the phone . . ." Her voice trailed off, and Marcus and I seemed to realize at about the same moment that this was not only business. It was personal.

"If you could excuse us, Mrs. Craig," the consultant said. "I would like to have a word with Eva." He still stood near the door, and I had my head turned over my shoulder looking at him.

The mayor put her hands on the desk top, managing to lean over and keep her back ramrod straight at the same time. "Marc, did I actually hear you dismiss someone from *my* office?"

He met her eyes. "It's Marcus. I haven't used Marc in years." He took a leather case from his pocket and withdrew a cream-colored business card. Eva did not reach out to take it, so he laid it on her desk.

"Oh, I forgot," she said. "You're Dr. Marcus Hillburn now, nationally known expert on budget cuts and school closures. I believe I read that."

"This doesn't have to be ugly, dear," he said, and I knew by his tone he had underestimated Eva.

She pushed her hair behind her ear, her sleek bob immaculate, her knit suit from the designer collection in her store a perfect fit. "Have a seat, then, and let's discuss how to work this out. Lois and I are eager to hear what you have to say. Aren't we, Lois?"

"By all means," I murmured, torn between running from the room before blood was shed and pulling up my chair for a closer look.

"I would prefer to speak with you in private," he said.

"And I would prefer that you get out of my office and out of my town and leave my school alone."

This felt like an elite tennis match, and I couldn't quite tell who was going to win the match. My eyes moved from one to the other.

"I owe you an apology," he said. "Several apologies, in fact. It was a terrible misunderstanding. I thought perhaps you'd rather not handle this in front of . . . well . . . in front of the owner of the local newspaper."

"I don't do off-the-record," Eva said, "even when the source is my ex-husband. Oh! Scratch that last sentence." She looked at me. "I meant to say, especially when the source is my ex-husband."

"You've changed after all, Eva," he said, trading his domineering consultant voice for a hushed, hurt tone.

"Thirty years and a husband's desertion will do that to a girl," she said.

My head flew back to Marcus. "The years have been kind to you," he said.

"Kinder to me than you were," she said.

As I again considered scrambling from the room, Dub popped in. He wore jeans, a denim shirt, and a pair of worn cowboy boots. He looked as cheerful as Marcus looked stern. "Evie, are you . . ."

To say Dub's voice trailed off would be like saying the Super Bowl is another football game or that it doesn't matter if a tornado hits on your wedding day. His mouth dropped so quickly that he almost looked like one of Chris's catfish. "I didn't realize you had guests," he said. "Louise was away from her desk."

"Evie?" Marcus said, repeating the nickname. "Evie?"

Suddenly Dub wasn't so chipper, transforming into the brusque businessman he had been when I bought the paper from his family.

"I don't believe we've met," he said, straightening his shoulders and extending his hand. "Dub McCuller."

Marcus hesitated long enough to be obvious and then pumped Dub's hand as though he were running for governor. "Dr. Marcus Hillburn," he said, with the emphasis on his last name.

"You're that fellow who came in here to tell us how to run our school," Dub said. "Can't say that it's all that nice to meet you. Lois, your husband's Rabbits are having a mighty fine season, aren't they?"

"Yes, they are," I said. "They're playing extra hard for Anthony."

"Joe and I went by yesterday to do a few maintenance chores for that young man's family, and he was working with a home-health therapist."

Marcus and Eva both listened to our conversation, and I tried to figure out what was going to happen before I got out of this room.

"Mayor," Dub said, finally turning from me to Eva. "I wanted to tell you I took care of that matter you asked about."

"Thank you, Dub," she said. "I'll be in touch in a few minutes. Maybe you could show Marc the way out. He was just leaving."

While I would have folded after that collision of past and present, Eva was reenergized, with a bit more sparkle in her eyes than usual.

"I'd like to hear what those two say to each other," I said, as soon as they left the office.

"I hope Dub's making up a tale about an important business deal under way and not telling that he took Sugar Marie to get her toenails trimmed and painted," Eva said, with what from any other woman I knew would have been a giggle. "That Marc is one smug piece of work, isn't he?"

"Looks that way," I said. "I wanted to take notes on how you handled him."

"I've learned a few things since I let him sweep me off my feet. But I'd rather not use those skills."

"It can't be easy dealing with him after so many years."

"It's hard," she agreed. "I thought I'd erased him from my life, and seeing him again stings." She fiddled with her pen. "I feel disloyal to Dub admitting that, though."

"You were married to Marcus. How could you ever forget him?" Even though Chris and I hadn't been married a year, I couldn't imagine not having him in my life.

"Our marriage wasn't like yours," she said, as though reading my thoughts. "Marc's ego and image were much more important to him than I was. He broke my heart years ago, but he won't do it again."

She pulled out a yellow legal pad. "You're a good listener, Lois."

"Me?"

"Don't look so surprised," Eva said. "We've wasted enough time talking about the esteemed Dr. Hillburn. What must we do to keep our school open?"

Despite her words, her voice was not quite as resolute as usual, and her hand shook as she picked up her pen. The encounter had taken more out of her than she wanted to let on.

"Eva, we don't have to discuss this right now." I tried to lighten the atmosphere. "You might need to check on the color Dub chose for Sugar's nails."

She took a deep breath, gave what I considered one of her politician smiles, and transitioned back to the Eva I knew so well. "I am more than up to this challenge, and we don't have any time to spare. You heard what he said. We have three months to do what you and I both know is nearly impossible."

I respected her too much to dwell on the personal dynamics of this situation, so I shifted gears.

"Let's start with the money," I said. "How are they paying for this consultant? Why did they target our town? Are things as dire as they're making them out to be?"

"Our students tend to be poor, and they don't test well," she said. "Our story is not so different from that of many towns in many states. I take responsibility for this situation."

"You're the mayor, not the school superintendent. The *Item* should have investigated this. I learned how to track all of these trends at the paper in Dayton. Why didn't I do a better job here?"

"You can't do everything."

"But I could have done more."

We were trying to help each other feel better, both of us feeling as though we had let Green down.

"We're moving forward, Lois," Eva said. "I am. You are. Now, if you'll excuse me, I believe I'll surprise Marc with a call and see what I can ferret out."

Marcus Hillburn's face and the image of a ferret melded perfectly in my mind.

10

*The We're Not Old group's weekly gathering abruptly
came to a halt when 95-year-old Mamie Sizemore lost
control of her 1981 Buick and ran off the road, over the
curb and into a yard next door to where the meeting was
held. No one was hurt, but members were pretty shaken
up. Miss Mamie says she didn't see the curb and was
only trying to find a parking space.*

—The Green News-Item

We need to talk about this school situation," Chris said.

The dogs ran ahead as we walked hand-in-hand late one evening. A warm snap had interrupted winter and hinted at spring, but my husband's words had a chill to them. The school might as well have been a third person in our new marriage because it certainly went everywhere we did.

"Are you worried?" I asked.

"You know I'm not a worrier, but I'm also not foolish. This may be a lost cause."

"Surely you don't mean that." I stopped on the gravel road and turned to stare, trying to read his expression. The thin sliver of a moon shone in the winter sky but didn't provide enough light for me to tell much.

"Maybe we need to plan for a school merger and help lead others through the transition," he said.

"Green deserves its own school," I said. "It's not right for outsiders to take that away."

"Would it be that bad?"

"This doesn't sound like you," I said.

His tone was grim when he spoke again, and he looked rugged in the worn plaid flannel shirt and ancient canvas jacket he had rescued from his parents' attic after his clothes blew away. "I need to say something you probably aren't going to like."

"Way to ruin a mood," I joked and squeezed his hand. "It never goes well when someone says that."

"It would be a lot easier on both of us if you'd step back from this situation," he said.

"You're not serious?"

He bent over and picked up a small rock and tossed it down the road. The dogs, barking loudly, chased it like it was alive. Mannix, who had lost a leg in the tornado, fell back a little, as though waiting for Holly Beth, who had trouble keeping up with Markey and Kramer.

"I know the paper has to cover the story," he said, "but everything's complicated."

"You're actually suggesting I retreat from the biggest story ever to hit Green?"

"I thought the tornado was the biggest story ever." He stuck his hands back in his jacket pockets. "Before that it was your investigation of Major Wilson and his corruption. Then Chuck McCuller set fires and tried to run you out of town. It's always something, Lois."

"What happened to 'you do your job, and I'll do mine'?" I asked, reaching over to pet Mannix and Holly, who had run back to us and were trying to outdo each other for attention. The bigger dogs sniffed in the ditch, their tails wagging as they explored every inch.

"I know you have to do your job," Chris said. "I'm suggesting you do it differently. You've laid the groundwork. Maybe it's time to let Iris or Linda take the reins on this one."

"That would be like asking you to assign one of your assistants to coach the championship game." I stuffed my hands in the pockets of my fleece-lined denim coat, a Christmas present from my family in Ohio. "If we roll over and play dead, the school might as well have blown away."

"It's not that I don't want the paper to cover the story," he said. "It's just that when you go near Priscilla, it's like gasoline and fire, and that makes things even tenser at work. Do you have to be the one to lead this fight?"

"I'm not leading the fight. I'm the messenger. I'm doing my best to get along with Priscilla, but Green deserves a school. If the paper doesn't save it, I don't know who will."

"I'm proud of you and what your paper does," Chris said, pulling me into the warmth of his arms, "but maybe it's time we let someone else fight these battles."

"Is that the choice you want to make?"

"I hate to see you work so hard and get hurt by one more problem in Green."

"Hurt?" I said. "All the problems led me right to my wonderful husband and taught me not to give up."

"You truly believe we can make a difference in how this school closing turns out, don't you?"

"There's so much riding on it. I have faith that we can make this better."

"What if it doesn't work? Maybe the students would be happy once they settled in."

"That's possible," I said. "If it doesn't work out, we'll know the decisions were made for the right reasons—and that we gave it our best."

"I'm with you all the way." Chris kissed me firmly and peered into my eyes. "I'll be glad, though, when we can spend our time and energy on other things. I enjoy working on the house with you. Our house. Me and you."

"Me, too," I said, cuddling up against him. "Did you see how great that trim looks in the guestroom?"

"The best part of the whole project is watching you when the crew finishes something. That makes you happy, doesn't it?"

"You make me happy, Chris, but you're trying to do too much."

"Those words are scary coming from the woman who takes on the entire town." He linked his fingers through mine, his hand warm in the cold air. "We sure could use a few easy months." He slipped his arm around my waist.

"That would be nice," I said.

———

"She refused to talk to me," Linda said, throwing her tote bag onto a chair. "Can she get away with that?"

"She threw Linda out of her office." Tammy huffed into my office on the reporter's heels.

I looked up, trying to shift from research on small school districts to the outraged look on both their faces. I didn't have time to say anything before Linda continued. "Tell me again how to find that law on the public's right to know."

"Sunshine laws," Tammy said. "I'm going to call Walt."

I held up my hand. "Wait a minute. I'm not following either of you."

"That new principal told Linda the school doesn't have to talk to the press," Tammy said.

"She escorted me off the school property," Linda said at the same time. "Said if I came back, she'd have me arrested."

"Are you telling me that Pricilla Robinson banned you from campus?"

"Not me. Us. All of us at the *Item*." Linda looked as though she were about to step into the ring at a boxing match. "I told her I had not been a reporter very long, but I knew enough to know she couldn't get away with that." She gave a small smile. "I was bluffing, of course."

"Technically, she probably can keep us off school property," I said.

After a conference call with Walt, in his official role as First Amendment attorney, the three of us looked at each other in dismay.

"When I worked for Major at the real estate office, he used to tell me newspapers had it easy," Linda said. "I didn't have a clue how hard it was for you to do your job. What do we do now?"

"You heard Walt," I said. "We can either file a request for public records or we can try to change Priscilla's mind and get the info from her."

"We use honey," Tammy muttered.

"What in the world are you talking about?"

"We use honey, instead of vinegar," Tammy said.

"You have to talk to her, Lois," Linda said, "appeal to her ego."

"That's not going to happen." I shook my head so hard it strained my neck. "I tried that with Chuck McCuller, and it didn't work. He laughed in my face and tried to take the paper back."

"You tell us we have to keep trying," Tammy said. "Why is this different?"

I sighed. "I don't know which I like less—when you listen to me or when you don't."

～∞∞∞～

A student worker answered the first time I called and took my name, sounding every bit as professional as a seasoned receptionist. However, when she put me on hold, there was a clatter as though she had dropped the receiver, and the call went dead.

When I hit redial, the line was busy, and by the time I got through, the teenage secretary sounded a bit frazzled. "The principal had to go to a meeting," she said. "Could someone else help you?"

The girl, a senior who had been one of Katy's buddies, sounded so remorseful that I apologized for not calling back sooner, left my number, and hung up as other lines rang in the background.

By the time school let out, I was not feeling nearly so charitable. "Are you sure she got my messages?" I asked when the only full-time office employee picked up the phone.

"Absolutely," she said. "I put all six of them on her desk myself."

"Did you tell her it was important that I speak with her before the paper comes out?"

The woman, whose son played for Chris, sighed. "I did."

"Did she say anything?"

"Not exactly." She hesitated. "It's possible she rolled her eyes."

"I heard voices in the background."

"Would you like to speak to Mr. Ellis instead? He just came in." Relief flowed through the woman's voice.

Without waiting for my answer, she murmured, and the former principal spoke next. "Is there a problem, Lois?"

"Priscilla won't return my calls. What's that all about?"

His sigh sounded louder than the clerk's. "I appreciate your zeal, but everything that needs saying has been said."

"So you've known they were going to force you out and close the school?" I asked.

He cleared his throat. "No."

"You can't spring something like this on people and expect them to smile and move along."

"I agree," he said. "But that doesn't make any difference. I don't have any pull with the school board since that fancy consultant came to town. With Priscilla's help, he's got them eating out of the palm of his hand, letting them think they made the decision."

"He certainly is confident," I said.

"It's easy to be confident when you never doubt you could be wrong. That's not for publication, by the way. I don't need to get fired right here before retirement. Let me see if I can get the principal for you."

I scanned through my notes while I waited for Priscilla, but it was Eugene's voice that came on the phone. "Miss Robinson said to fax your questions, and she'll answer them when she can."

"What?"

"She has her own way of doing things," he said. "For a young person, she's set in her ways."

"You know a principal can't avoid the local paper, Eugene. It comes with the territory."

"I've tried to tell her that."

After the call ended, I fumed, fidgeted with paperwork, and examined the list of possible ways to save the school. Finally I grabbed my purse and jacket and headed through the lobby.

"I've had it with that bureaucratic pencil-pushing principal," I said to Tammy, who was choosing wedding and anniversary photographs for that week's bridal pages. "I'm going to her office."

"Hmmm." She hit save on the computer and turned toward me. "Didn't you tell us you had decided to let Linda handle the visits to the school?"

"I refuse to let this woman stonewall the newspaper. The citizens have a right to know."

Driving to the campus, I wondered if I was hurting Chris by confronting his boss. After our discussion a few nights earlier, I had decided I owed my husband a compromise—that the paper had to do full coverage but I would stay behind the scenes.

That didn't seem to be working.

The school grounds were nearly empty by the time I arrived, with a few vehicles, including my husband's pickup, parked near the gymnasium. Maria, the woman Chris had given his mobile home to when we married, pushed a large dust mop in the first-floor hallway. I could practically see my reflection in the shiny old green tile.

"Hola, Miss Lois," she said in her lyrical voice.

"Hi, Maria. How are your boys?"

"Pastor Jean has them this afternoon. She lets them play at her house until I get off from work." She attended the Spanish-language service at Grace Chapel and took English lessons downtown. Her accent was strong, but her vocabulary had improved greatly in the last year.

"Are they enjoying school?" I asked.

A smile, followed by a frown, ran across her face. "Very much, especially the baby. He goes to . . ." She searched for the word. ". . . pre-kindergarten, but if they close the school, I do not know what I will do."

"Try not to worry," I said.

As I walked off, she was on her hands and knees, scraping gum off the floor.

No one was in the school office, so I stuck my head in the principal's door, the larger office Priscilla had evicted Mr. Ellis from.

Eugene and Marcus Hillburn were arguing when I entered, and Priscilla had a sour look on her face. Seeing me did not make matters better.

"Are you looking for your husband?" she asked.

"I hoped to have a word with you."

"As you can see, I am tied up," she said. "Perhaps another time."

Eugene stood up, welcoming the interruption. "I think we've about done all the damage we can do today," he said with a false chuckle. He wore the same weary look that Chris had most evenings. "I'll see you at the game tonight."

"I expect those numbers by tomorrow," Priscilla said, and I tried to hide my anger at the lack of respect in her tone.

"I'll see what I can do." Mr. Ellis left the room with a pained look.

Marcus started to stand, but Priscilla gave a quick shake of her head, and he sat back down. Having watched her sink her fangs into Eugene, I was happy to take on both of them.

"I only have a few questions," I said. "Perhaps Dr. Hillburn can help me if you aren't available."

"The two of us are involved in a meeting," she said. She stumbled over the word "involved" and momentarily lost her ice-cold composure. "As I told that reporter of yours today, I have no comment and will not allow the media to disrupt our daily business."

Marcus cast his eyes from Priscilla back to me, then seemingly scrutinized his slacks, another pair with a perfect crease.

I acted as though I were spellbound by the principal, trying to be polite when everything in me wanted to be patronizing.

"I'm on deadline, Priscilla," I said. "I very much need your perspective."

She leaned toward the desk, looked at her watch, and then back at me.

"Have a seat," she said, "and let Dr. Hillburn and me walk you through what's going on." Her words were spoken in the tone she might have used with a second-grader.

"Everyone wants what's best for the children," Priscilla said for the thousandth time since this debate had begun. "While it would be great for Green to keep its quaint little school, that is not feasible."

I pulled a notebook out of my purse. "May I?" I held up my pen, and she nodded. I wrote down her quotes.

"We do not have enough money to keep this school open forever," she said. "Avoiding action now only delays the inevitable."

"But what about the attention and education students get in a small school?" My voice was calm.

Marcus looked at Priscilla, and once more she nodded, clearly giving him permission to speak. "You don't understand," he said. "Even when Green merges, the new school will still be small in the eyes of the state."

"Beyond that," the woman interrupted, "just because students attend a friendly little rural school doesn't mean they're getting a good education."

"Why not lobby for another year for the school," I asked, "and see what we can come up with? What do you get out of shutting us down?"

The two exchanged a glance, and the principal stood. "This is an emotional issue. Unlike most of Green, Dr. Hillburn and I are not hysterical in our approach."

"There's a difference between affection for your community and hysteria," I said. "It's easy to hit and run, but it might be more worthwhile to roll up your sleeves and make the school better."

"Once more, Ms. Craig, it sounds like you think you can do my job better than I can." Priscilla herded me toward the door as she spoke. "Maybe you'd better stick to your little newspaper."

Speechless, I looked her up and down, wondering how someone so young could be so arrogant. At the look on Marcus Hillburn's face, I knew she had learned at least part of it from him.

Striding out of the office, I turned the corner and ran full force into Chris. I braced myself for his scolding.

"I tried to step back. I really did," I said before he could speak.

"I'm glad to see you," he said.

"You're not mad at me for coming over here again?"

He shook his head. "I heard Priscilla and Marcus were hateful to Linda. I figure you're the only one who knows how to handle them when push comes to shove."

I nodded toward the principal's office. "I thought I might butter Priscilla up."

"How'd that work out for you?" Chris asked, a twinkle in his eye.

"About the way it worked when you tried to talk your father out of those chickens."

11

*Cora Johnson was eight years old when she won a fancy
doll at the Beulah Missionary Church raffle. Now the
Centenary College graduate is headed to Indonesia as
a full-time missionary, and the doll is being raffled
again—this time to raise funds for the trip. The 20-inch,
red-haired doll has green eyes, rosy cheeks and a
custom-made wardrobe created by Cora's aunt,
well-known local seamstress Ellie Melancon. Raffle
tickets are available at the church, and, lest you think of
this as gambling, remember it is for a good cause.*

—*The Green News-Item*

On the first day of worship in the new Grace Community
Chapel, to quote most of the residents of Route Two: "The bottom fell out."

It rained so hard that members sat in their cars waiting for
it to let up, puddles forming in the unpaved parking lot. Some
people turned plastic grocery sacks into rain gear and wrestled
with covered dishes, sloshing their way to the back door, near
the new kitchen.

"So much for the grand parade into the sanctuary," I said to
Chris, digging around for my umbrella. "I was looking forward
to the children leading us in."

With rain hammering on the roof of his old pickup, his
windshield wipers barely kept up, but my husband's voice was

positive. "We'll have other sunny days. Let's go inside and celebrate what that building committee of yours came up with."

Pastor Jean's smile wiped away my disappointment.

Standing inside the front door, a cold wind blowing rain in with each person, she looked happier than I had ever seen her.

"Remember your baptism," she said with a laugh and gave me a damp hug.

Members and guests huddled in the back of the sanctuary, drying off, chatting loudly, and trying to figure out what to do with their umbrellas. The old church had a foyer, the perpetual location of faded umbrellas, lost jackets, and forgotten Bibles, but we decided the space could be better used as one big room. Immediately I realized we had never once discussed where umbrellas would go.

For a second I felt like a visitor, even though I had helped plan the facility and knew all the particulars of the dedication service.

Everything was so different.

The walls were painted a rich cream color, and only one of the old stained glass windows had been installed. The others were in storage, warped and in need of expert restoration. Instead the windows were an opaque pearl color, to let light in but keep distractions out. The smell of the space heater in the fellowship hall was gone, replaced by the even warmth of central heat.

I glanced down at my wet shoes and at the floor. "At least we don't have to worry about ruining the carpet," I said.

"This linoleum was a good choice," Chris said. "We need something that can handle wear and tear."

"It's not linoleum," I said with mock outrage. "Linoleum was what you had in your old trailer. This, I'll have you know, is top-of-the-line vinyl floor covering."

We weren't the only ones standing back observing, critiquing, and trying to get a feel for the new place. All around us members and a few visitors pointed and commented, most in English and a few in Spanish, participants from our service for the large Hispanic population in Green.

"Where will we sit?" I heard one elderly member ask her husband.

"Where we always sit," he said.

"But we've never been in here before . . ." Her voice trailed off, and she followed him to the front left, the location they had occupied in the old wooden building.

Chris grabbed my hand and grinned. "It'll feel like home in no time. Are we sticking with the back row, or do you want to choose a new location?"

The spot where I first landed in Grace Chapel, as an observer and not participant, looked appealing, but that wasn't the place for me any longer. Chris had never been a fan of the back row, and I was in the middle of things at the church, even though I had not intended to be.

"Let's sit with your parents," I said, steering him to the right. He gave me such a big smile that I wanted to kiss him right there. In his church slacks and wearing a rare tie, he was so handsome that I still couldn't believe he had married me.

Making our way to Estelle and Hugh Craig, we were hugged and greeted so many times that the opening music started before we sat down. My in-laws seemed surprised and delighted as we took our seats. "I thought I'd miss the pews," Estelle whispered, "but these chairs are comfortable."

One of the things I loved about my mother-in-law was her ability to see the bright side in anything. She had passed much of that along to Chris, whose calm optimism had invaded my life before I even realized it.

"I'll admit I had my concerns about a metal building," I said, "but the details worked out well."

"It's a happy space," Estelle said. "And you look so pretty today. I like that blue shirt with your dark hair." Had I worn a flour sack, she would still have complimented me, but her words reminded me of my mother and moved me.

The chatter stopped abruptly, and a sense of anticipation filled the space—or maybe it was only filling my heart. It felt like something good was about to happen. The choir director pounded out a triumphant hymn on the old piano, one of the few things to survive water damage after the tornado.

Playing with exuberance, Mary Frances nodded to the choir, seated on the front rows, and they filed up to the front. A few members were still disgruntled about the lack of a true choir loft, but the musicians looked sharp in their new blue robes with gold collars and smiled as they scanned the crowded room.

While they took their places, Pastor Jean led the processional of children up the center aisle, each child carrying a new Bible. As the music stopped, the hush felt like you could reach out and touch it.

The heavy rain pounded on the roof, and I was certain I wasn't the only person remembering the last time many of us had gathered in the old church, the night Chris and I married. The rain that night had been the harbinger of the tornado that took the church building from us.

My father-in-law stood and walked to the back of the church, and Joe Sepulvado, wearing a coat and tie, moved to join him.

Mr. Sepulvado, who had barely survived the horrible storm, insisted we find a way to move the heavy, pewter church bell. Hugh, who had rung the bell since he was a boy, suggested that since he was nearly as old as the bell Joe should take over the weekly tradition.

Most of the church twisted around to see what was going on.

Hugh stood at attention, as though preparing to sing the national anthem, and the other man, a migrant farm worker from Mexico, solemnly pulled the rope. The sound of the ringing was deep and melodious.

Without a word, the congregation stood, and tears flowed down the faces of many, my own included.

As the last gong faded, Hugh and Joe shook hands and headed to their seats.

A new tradition had begun.

"God, our God," Pastor Jean said, speaking from a lectern instead of a pulpit, "we know you are here with us, as you were in the old building and are wherever we come together in Your name. We offer this building to you as we gather to worship and celebrate grace and forgiveness. Amen."

"Amen," the congregation repeated and settled in to listen to Jean. Her husband, Don, who worked in Baton Rouge during the week, sat right up front.

Today the preacher stood before us without the robe and stole she had worn in the old building. The decision to pack those away had pleased some and bothered others. Wearing a long knit skirt and blouse and a pair of serviceable pumps, she looked like a cross between a professor and an insurance agent.

Her words left no doubt she was a pastor.

"We left our old location in rain, and we christen this building in rain," she said. "No matter how old you are or how young, what your job or how much money you have—or don't have, in many of our cases . . ." The congregation laughed, and the sense of being at home spread deeper within me.

"Whatever our Lord does here will be done through our hands and feet, our hearts." Jean's voice sounded as bold as Mary Frances pounding out a hymn on the piano.

As Jean finished, the youth choir, consisting of eight teens and a half dozen elementary students, stood to the side and sang a medley of contemporary praise songs, with the girl Randi, whom I had seen in the school office, playing a keyboard.

Trying to decide what other members were thinking, I was shocked to see the older couple who had entered in front of us stand and walk to the aisle. Were they leaving?

They did not, however, walk to the back of the church, as I had thought. They went to the front and knelt.

Slowly, one by one, people filed to the front and knelt to pray or stood with heads bowed.

Maria, who lived in what had been Chris's old trailer, held hands with her three sons as she walked forward, a beautiful smile on her face and the boys looking subdued, as though they knew something important was happening but weren't quite sure what.

Pastor Jean stepped down to welcome the trio, who had become like family to her, and I remembered the day I slipped into the battered Grace Chapel for the last time, the day I knew we would never worship there again. That building was so quaint it looked like a painting in a picture book, and Maria had eased the pain of saying farewell, greeting me from across the road, her boys playing in the yard.

With music playing quietly, the youth turned and bowed together. Chris took my hand, and we made our way to the front, Hugh and Estelle putting their hands on our shoulders as we knelt.

The scent of lilies from the altar spray, designed and delivered by Becca, the florist down the street from the paper, met my nose. The sound of sniffling could be heard over the calm music, and several older gentlemen fumbled for their handkerchiefs. I wished I had thought to bring tissues.

The irony of my feelings was not lost on me. "I'm not much of a churchgoer," I had told Iris Jo and several others when I moved to town. I used excuses of a busy schedule, my temporary status in Green and my overall lack of interest in getting involved. But something drew me to the church, and I had felt myself thaw.

Today I could almost see the spirit of God in this metal building, and I smiled at how I had changed.

Within moments of worship, the new sanctuary was transformed into a fellowship hall of sorts, tables set up and chairs rearranged. The youth and an assortment of men laughed and visited as they set up the new tables, and members of the new "Gathering Committee" whisked out tablecloths and centerpieces, pink and red camellias from bushes in nearby yards, each with shiny, dark-green leaves.

A hefty roster of visitors joined us for the meal afterwards, including pastors from other churches in town and Mayor Eva, who slipped in after her own church's service and made her way to Pastor Jean. As the two women greeted each other, I noticed Dub get up from his seat next to Joe Sepulvado and load an extra plate of food from the potluck assortment.

He caught Eva's eye, held the plate up, and then set it on the table, making a trip to the big cooler of tea and trays of plastic forks and knives. The mayor smiled, gave an almost imperceptible nod of her head, and continued working her way around the room. While many in the room were still a bit damp, she looked as though she had stepped out of the hairdresser's chair a moment before, her clothes as fresh as if they had just come from the dry cleaners.

"What a lovely building," she said, giving me one of her standard half hugs, not the hearty embrace of many Green residents but well beyond the handshakes I had gotten from politicians in Dayton. "Your congregation has created something special here, so beautiful but functional, too."

She waved her hand at the space. "Did you actually have church here a few minutes ago?"

"Hard to believe, isn't it?" I gestured around the room. "We made a fresh start today, but we kept many of the traditions from the old church. I wish you could have heard the bell. Joe Sepulvado rang it, and there wasn't a dry eye in the house."

"And not because of the rain," Dub said, walking up behind Eva.

The two acknowledged each other in an oddly personal way without speaking a word, and I looked away for a moment, searching for Chris.

"Lois, your committee did an outstanding job," Dub said. "Joe tells me you were a leader all the way."

"Joe and others did the hard work. My role was to raise questions about how to best use the space, and they answered all those and then some."

"This project helped take Joe's mind off the loss of his wife," Dub said. "I told him if he kept working so many hours over here, I was going to have to give him a curfew."

"So he's still living with you?" I asked. Joe had moved in with Dub after the tornado destroyed his travel trailer and killed his wife. Almost dead himself, he was rescued by Chris's dog Mannix.

"For as long as I can convince him to stay," Dub said. "I have plenty of room, and my Spanish is improving every day."

"As is Joe's English," Eva said. "You're doing a great job as a tutor."

Following a few more moments of chatting, the mayor walked off with Dub, settling in to the plate of food after he held the chair out for her. I thought for a moment he would place the napkin in her lap, too. He bent to talk to Joe, and all three laughed.

"Still can't quite let him off the hook, can you?" I jumped as Chris appeared next to me.

"I'm trying to," I said. "Everyone acts like he never did anything wrong. I'd rather not run into him every time I turn around."

"He's been good to Joe and a big help with the food program. Eva seems to have forgiven him."

"Dub and his brother were world class bullies, and he'll have to earn my trust."

"I think that's what he's doing." Chris grabbed my hand. "Let's get a plate. I don't want to miss Mama's sweet potato pie."

The line wound around the room, and I looked for a spot to sit. My eyes widened as they rested on Priscilla Robinson and Marcus Hillburn, chatting with Katy's mother and stepfather and a teacher or two who worked at Green High.

"What are they doing here?" I muttered.

Chris turned from the green-bean casserole and shrugged. "Going to church? Eating lunch?"

"Don't you think it's odd that out of all the churches in Green they'd choose Grace?"

"Not particularly. We are having a community celebration today. Half the town has wandered in, and they like to be seen out and about. You know that."

"Looks to me like they're trying to get in good with the school administration. They drop a bomb and try to act like they're our friends."

"Lois, you tell everyone how welcoming Grace Chapel is. Come one, come all, remember?"

I picked up an olive from a relish tray and popped it into my mouth.

"Quit fretting, and give thanks for this new building." Chris softened his words with the grin that could warm my heart on the coldest day.

I looked around the room and knew. Grace was offered to all, whether I liked them or not.

12

Patricia McGuire says thanks to everyone for their
support at the near-death of Pal, her sweet Chihuahua,
after the sugar-free gum incident. "Tell everyone they
are not to give their dogs such a treat under any
circumstance," she said. "The vet's assistant
told me I should have known better."

—The Green News-Item

Katy loved college, but she could hardly stand being away from the action in Green.

"Did readers like my opinion piece about being a Rabbit?" she asked one afternoon. She had started calling every day and asking us to put her on the speaker phone in the newsroom.

We glided in and out of the conversation, almost as though she were in the room.

The habit had replaced what Linda called "newsroom happy hour," when Tom concentrated on a crossword puzzle and the rest of us wrapped up the day's work and joked around. I leaned back on the scratchy sofa to the side of the room and watched each of my employees, thinking about how much I enjoyed them.

"Katy, grads loved your column," Molly said. "That e-mail campaign was a great idea. At least seventy-five percent of our class voiced opposition to closing the school. Have you read their comments? They're awesome."

"That e-mail deal was my marketing professor's idea," Katy said. "She said it's a perfect example of how businesses can interact with customers."

"Good thing Tom can't hear you say that," Tammy chimed in, her feet propped on a desk, a half-eaten granola bar in her hand. "He'd say that's a public service, not a business move."

"Can't it be both?" Linda asked, not looking up from her computer.

"We're a business," Tammy said. "But we've got responsibilities, too. Walt and I were talking last night at supper about why we have the First Amendment. We're supposed to use those protections for good."

"That sounds like what a superhero would say," Katy said.

"You're talking about the U.S. Constitution over supper?" I said. "I think Chris and I were debating whether Ginger or Mary Ann was cuter on 'Gilligan's Island.'"

The conversation meandered on, a blend of current events and girl talk. Linda closed the story she was working on and opened another file, rarely wasting a minute.

"You're not saying much today, Lois," Katy said.

"She's not sure what to do about the school coverage," Molly said, as though I weren't in the room.

"She's keyed up," Tammy added.

"I am not," I said. "OK, maybe I'm wound a little tight over this. It's not easy covering a story that involves your husband."

"Tell me about it," Katy said. "My mom says my stepdad is like a bear with a sore paw. He's between a rock and a hard place."

"He's the one who put the rock there," I said. "Chris got caught in the fallout. He's losing sleep over what this is doing to teachers and students."

"My stepfather hopes the paper will manage to change the school board's mind."

"Fat chance," I said.

"In case you can't tell, she's frowning," Tammy said.

Katy went on. "He can't say too much, since he's the superintendent, but he's waiting for the *Item* to pull a trick out of its sleeve."

"How about he comes up with something, and we write about it?" I said. "I'm fresh out of ideas."

Tammy made a "tsking" sound. "I can hear James now. 'Don't ever underestimate Lois Barker Craig.'"

Everyone but me laughed, and the topic turned to whether Katy should let her hair grow out and how much she should spend on a new pair of jeans.

Molly rummaged around on Tom's desk, pulled out a yellowed newspaper page, and walked over to the copy machine. "Have you heard from Alex since the big fight?" she asked.

"What fight?" Tammy and I asked at the same time.

"Molly," Katy wailed. "I told you not to tell anyone."

"I didn't think you meant these people," her friend said. "You tell them everything. Besides, they worked with Alex, too. It isn't any big secret that you're seeing each other."

"I go to college in Georgia, and he works in Idaho," Katy said. "We're not exactly seeing each other."

"Whatever," Molly said.

"Now you're rolling your eyes, aren't you?" her friend said. "You let the cat out of the bag about Alex, and now you're acting like I'm stupid."

"What was the fight with Alex about?" I jumped in to break up their bickering.

"Alex said if Katy's stepfather won't be more forthcoming that the newspaper should dig deeper," Molly said, "or file a lawsuit."

"James has always shot straight with the *Item*," I said. "I don't sense he's trying to hide anything."

Katy's dramatic sigh could be heard through the phone. "Of course he's not hiding anything. Ever since that exposé on Major Wilson, Alex thinks he's a hot-shot investigative reporter and there's a secret around every corner."

"He did get Major sent to jail and won a state award for that project," Linda said. "Maybe we should listen to him."

"Mr. James wouldn't break a rule for any reason," Molly said. "He tells me and Katy all the time to live by a personal code of honor."

"Don't ever do anything you're ashamed of," the two girls chanted in unison.

"I'll wait for y'all to figure all this out. I've got chemistry lab and need to grab my books," Katy said. "I love you guys."

"We love you, too," Molly said. "Call me later."

The room grew quiet after the call, and I looked from woman to woman. "What are we missing? Could the school board be hiding something?"

Linda flipped through her files. "I can't shake the feeling that there's more to this than meets the eye."

"Don't forget that the school numbers haven't been good for a while," Iris said. "We aren't graduating the students we should or testing as well as we need to."

"Wow," Tammy said. "Are you secretly an investigative reporter?"

"I'm a numbers person," Iris said. "I was worried when Matt started high school, and so I did lots of research. I suggested the story to Chuck, but he said it would turn off advertisers."

She gave a sad shrug. "When Matt was killed, it didn't seem important anymore."

"Do you still have that data?" I asked.

Tammy snorted. "That's like asking Molly if she likes that car of hers. Iris Jo has files going back to the turn of the century."

"The amazing thing is she can put her hands on all of them," Linda said, her eyes meeting mine, the pieces of a puzzle almost obvious as they came together in her mind. "Would you walk me through those, Iris?"

"Sure. But right now I'd better walk through that door and get back to our budget."

Linda settled back at her desk, her brow furrowed as she studied a thick file lying open in front of her.

Molly gathered up her backpack, preparing to leave for her second job at the Pak-N-Go.

I walked over to the page layouts in the composing area, and Tammy followed me.

"By the way, *do* you have a trick up your sleeve to save the school?" she asked.

"Not the last time I looked." I picked up a blue highlighter and pretended to be intent on classified advertising proofs.

Linda sighed. "We're missing something."

"Such as?" I asked, frustrated.

"Remember how I dated the biggest jerks in Green?" she asked.

"How could we forget?" Tammy said, never hesitant to jump into a juicy conversation.

Linda was an attractive woman in her mid-thirties whose life had been punctuated by a series of bad decisions. Buying into Rose's antique mall across the street and becoming a key part of the *Item* staff after a horrible job at Major Wilson's real-estate business had improved things for her.

"You made a mistake or two," I said. "I don't see what that has to do with this story."

"Not one of those guys was what he looked like on the surface," Linda said. "They acted like they had money and wanted to be with me . . . and then they turned out to be something totally different."

"I'm not following you," I said.

"I am," Tammy said, excited. "It's like me and my high school diploma. Everyone assumed I was a graduate, so they never considered I might be different than I seemed."

Molly rushed into the newsroom the next afternoon, backpack slung over her shoulder, a pair of sweat pants and athletic shoes on instead of her usual jeans and worn loafers.

I was looking through Tammy's collection of reader photos from past school events and didn't say anything, but Tammy looked surprised. "Going casual today?" she asked.

"Every day's casual day around here," I muttered.

Molly ignored the comments. "How far is it to Baton Rouge?" she asked.

Tammy cut her eyes to the teen. "For a college student, you may not know as much as I thought. Have you already forgotten your geography lessons?"

"I mean how long would it take to walk there?"

"Let's see," Tammy pretended to calculate. "The last time I tried that, I'd say it took me about two weeks."

"Tough classes today?" I asked.

"This doesn't have anything to do with school," she said, her tone similar to the one Katy used when we were too slow for her. "Not with my college classes, anyway."

I turned from the large stack of photos, a number of them one-of-a-kind snapshots of long-ago events, the students now grown. Although I recognized a few faces from the community, there were many I'd never seen before.

She dropped her pack on the floor by Tom's desk and picked up a yellowed newspaper page. Even though nearly a year had passed since Tom had died in the tornado, we could not bring ourselves to clean the clutter away. Katy called it the "messy memorial" and it looked as though the veteran copy editor had stepped out for lunch rather than been killed trying to tell us danger was on the way.

"I'm going to walk to Baton Rouge," Molly said.

She held up the old page. "Like these people did back in the sixties. I'm not going to sit on my hands and do nothing. I'm going to march on the capitol."

"Good idea," Tammy muttered. "I think I'll fly to the moon."

"I'm serious," Molly said. "I'm going to take a stand."

I reached out and took the old article from her hand, one of many that Tom had kept within reach "for reference and reminders." The layout showed a crowd on the steps of the state capitol, police officers and dogs lining the edges, the governor standing in the door.

"That was one of the very first pages Tom designed," I said. "He was very proud of it."

Iris Jo walked in as I spoke and looked over my shoulder. "Tom said that was one of Louisiana's finest days, when the people took their pleas to the governor."

Tammy gave up trying to pretend she wasn't interested. "Walt's father says it's the day ordinary people realized they had a voice."

"You talk to your father-in-law about things like this?" I asked, temporarily distracted.

"I'm still trying to make my in-laws think I'm smarter than I am," she said. "Don't you talk to your father-in-law?"

"We talk about things like chickens."

"I thought you'd be more excited about my idea," Molly said.

"Tell us more," Iris said, stepping into her usual role of encourager.

"I want to walk to Baton Rouge and ask the governor to keep our school open. That school gave me opportunities I'd have never gotten anywhere else."

"Have you thought about picking up the phone and calling?" Tammy asked.

"I want to do something that matters," Molly said. "You're getting your GED, and Anthony's trying to learn how to walk again. My mother's working hard to keep our family fed. Katy's three states away, and she still managed to get our classmates fired up. Everyone's doing something but me."

"You go to college and work two jobs," I said. "Three if you count babysitting for Asa."

"And you tutor that girl down the street," Iris said.

"Katy's stepfather is waiting for someone to do something," Molly said. "I've got to step up."

"I'd call a 200-plus-mile walk stepping up, all right," Tammy said.

"I'm already training. Anthony is coaching me. He says if he can't walk, at least he can do this." She hesitated. "I'll have to miss work, but, Linda, I hope you'll lay out pages while I'm gone."

"I love the idea," Linda said. "You can report on it. Write a column or two. It'll set our newspaper apart. You can post a blog."

Molly's eyes took on a new sparkle. "Katy," she said, and started dialing. "I'm going to ask Katy to go with me."

I wondered how long it would take them to figure out this wasn't a good idea.

———— ✺ ————

After a thirty-minute call, Molly and Katy had hatched a plan for a mid-May march, when college classes would be over and the legislature in session. Tammy had signed on to take photos, and Linda had begun to map a route and figure out logistics.

Molly came outside where I was walking Holly Beth and spelled out their plans. Climbing into her massive car, she gave a jaunty wave, the most exuberance I'd seen her show since Anthony's injury.

"Wait till Coach Chris hears about this," she said.

"Wait," I said out loud, and Holly looked up at me and barked, as though she understood perfectly.

Before the car had disappeared from sight, Iris walked over, and we sat on one of the new downtown benches, paid for with donations from Green Forward merchants.

"You and I know they can't possibly do this," I said. "Maybe they'll figure that out on their own before I have to squelch it."

She frowned, a rare sight for Iris. "I think it's inspiring, that Molly would come up with this with all she has to deal with in her life."

"She doesn't have the time or money to do this. Why can't someone else come up with something?"

"You heard what Katy said yesterday. James thinks the paper can keep the school from closing." Iris reached down to pet Holly, who chewed on the toe of her shoe. "Maybe you should leave this one to them."

"Chris has finally come around about the paper digging into this story, but he might not be happy about us organizing a march on Baton Rouge."

"Lois, I've known Chris a long time. He expects you to do what you think best, and he'll support you in whatever way he can. He's just getting used to being married to the newspaper owner."

"I don't want everyone to get their hopes up that we'll save the school," I said, "and then disappoint them."

She gave one of her sweet Iris smiles. "You're the woman who taught Green how to believe in itself. Let's see what happens."

———— ∞∞∞ ————

I went back into the newsroom and looked through the box of reader photos, marveling at a rare shot of Elvis Presley performing in the school auditorium and a picture of students gathered around a black-and-white TV with rabbit ears, watching Neil Armstrong step out onto the surface of the moon.

In another shot, a young Eva Hillburn wore a marching band uniform, Dub in the background in khakis and a plaid shirt, similar to what he often still wore, and Chuck McCuller in a football uniform.

Leaving the box on the desk, I put Holly in her crate and paced around my office, trying to figure out what we were missing. How would a big paper handle this story?

A nearly forgotten conversation with Gina Stonecash ran through my mind. In town to report on the tornado, she had reminisced about a corporate conference on education. I hurried over to a dusty shelf lined with loose-leaf notebooks and scanned the titles.

The notebook marked "From the Newsroom to the Classroom: Covering Education for the Years Ahead" was jammed next to a community comprehensive plan and handouts from a leadership conference I had attended.

My feet propped on the desk, I read through the speakers' handouts and looked at notes I had jotted in the margins. The meeting seemed like another lifetime ago, and I read the roster, remembering my former colleagues and the Pulitzer Prize one had snagged with an investigation of standardized testing.

Flipping through the folder, I found a summary of the article, which had exposed teachers who helped students cheat on tests for better results. I wondered if numbers could be adjusted in the other direction. I also discovered a series on how to get students to attend school consistently.

Maybe these ideas could move us along, but first I needed to settle another issue.

I left Holly with Iris, who promised to drop her at our house, and headed for the school. Instead of walking to the principal's office, my feet turned toward the gymnasium. The sound of bouncing basketballs and laughter resonated through the door. Anthony sat in his wheelchair with a stopwatch, calling out times as teammates dashed up and down the court.

"Is Coach Chris around?" I shouted over the racket.

"He's over there," a boy yelled, gesturing around the corner.

A subdued student walked out of Chris's office as I walked in. The air was a mix of sweat and deodorant. Chris, his head down, studied something on his desk in the cluttered room, a repository for lost sports items, dusty trophies, and calendars of every athletic schedule for the past ten years.

"Got a few minutes, Coach?" I said. He looked up, a broad smile creasing his face.

"I didn't expect to see you this afternoon," he said, and the smile faded. "Are you here for a meeting?"

"Sort of," I said. "I need to talk to you."

"What's wrong?"

"I want to run something by you."

He looked dubious.

"I love you," I said. "I will always be on your team, no matter what. I'd walk away from the *Item* today before I'd let it come between us."

He moved to embrace me, still frowning ever so slightly. "Nothing will ever come between us. We're here for each other."

When one falls down . . .

"What were you talking to that kid about right before I came in?" I asked.

Chris stepped back and wrinkled his face. "His grades aren't so hot. I told him I'd help with some worksheets, and he promised to quit skipping class."

"I don't think I've seen him before. Is he on the basketball team?"

Chris shook his head. "He transferred in at mid-term. He's not an athlete."

"I saw Anthony out there," I said.

"He's doing a great job as a trainer. He keeps stats, and I hope he'll be out of that chair by the end of school . . ." His voice trailed off.

"You help everyone," I said.

"Those boys need me." He ran his hand through his dark hair. "Most of their lives are full of turmoil."

"You're a wonderful teacher," I wrapped my arms around his neck again and planted a kiss on the top of his Green Rabbits baseball cap.

"The paper's about to blow something up, isn't it?" he asked.

"Not exactly," I said, "but we're going to try a new approach to save the school, if it's OK with you."

"What can I do to help?" he asked.

13

The view from the Green water tower is good, but climbing up there is foolish. This correspondent mentions it as a warning to the seven youngsters up there Saturday night. Why didn't I call the law? Because I did the same thing on my first date in the 1950s, but that boy turned out to be a scoundrel. If I see you up there again, I'll call the sheriff.

—*The Green News-Item*

Our chicken and dumplings were still steaming when Marcus Hillburn strolled into the Cotton Boll Café, carrying a copy of *The Wall Street Journal* and wearing a starched shirt, minus his usual tie.

With Tammy and me in the booth nearest the door, there was no way to pretend we didn't see him, although it was tempting to try.

"Hello, Marcus," I said. "I didn't know you were back in town."

"Just drove in," he said, holding up the newspaper as though that were proof.

"Nice to see you again, Dr. Hillburn," Tammy said.

It was obvious he didn't remember ever having laid eyes on Tammy before, and I debated whether to bail him out or not. Finally, my manners gave in. "Tammy King's our chief photographer at the *News-Item,* and she also keeps the lobby under control."

"Oh, the gatekeeper," he said with what might have been considered a wolfish smile on a younger man. "You helped me with my subscription. I finally got that all straightened out, and it arrives right on schedule."

"I hope you're enjoying our school coverage," Tammy said. "We have lots more stories to come."

I kicked her under the table and picked up my fork, hoping she would quit talking and Marcus would move on.

"I haven't had time to catch up on your reporting, but I'm certain it's been useful."

"You should see the wonderful old photos we've collected," she continued. "They bring back the best memories."

"I'll look forward to those," he said. "And are you a Green grad, Ms. King?"

Instead of the question taking Tammy aback, she put on her biggest, most genuine smile. "I was one of those students who didn't make it. I'm studying for the GED now as part of the newspaper's program to help dropouts."

My eyes got big.

"Well, good luck." He scanned the room and slid into the only open spot, the booth next to us.

Tammy, whose back was to him, buttered her cornbread muffin, looking full of herself.

"GED program?" I whispered. "What were you thinking?"

She laid the bread on her saucer. "Molly's mother, Esther, is doing great on her practice tests, and Anthony's mom wants to study, too. I meant to mention that. Pastor Jean suggested several members of Grace Chapel who are interested, especially Maria. I estimate we'll graduate a dozen from this first group."

I didn't know if she was serious or not, but I didn't want to ask her when the Texas consultant was so clearly listening.

Before I could think of something else to say, she leaned over the table and threw her eyes at the door. "This should be interesting."

I turned in time to see Dub McCuller walk in the door, wearing a suit and tie and carrying a gift-wrapped package.

"Hey, Mr. Dub," the waitress called the second he stepped in. "I'll have a table for you in a jiffy."

"No hurry." He stepped back to wait and noticed us. And Marcus.

"Hello, Lois, Tammy," he said. "Marc."

The other man nodded and went back to reading his paper, as though it were the most captivating thing ever. "Join us," Tammy said. "Take a load off while you wait."

Tammy had forgiven Dub for his part in illegal dealings with the newspaper, and I was trying, for Eva's sake and because he seemed like a nicer man now that his brother was dead. "Have a seat," I said.

My photographer took a drink of iced tea and reached over to straighten Dub's tie. "You're mighty dressed up for a retired fellow," she said.

"I had a meeting with the judge. I finished my probation today. I'm officially a free man." He acted as though he might reach over and pat my hand but then pulled back. "I offer my apologies again for all the problems I caused."

"That's history," I said, and just like that my anger toward him disappeared. "We have more important things to worry about these days."

He cut his eyes behind him. "The school issue is absurd," he said a little too loudly. "Who ever heard of a town without a school?"

Marcus stood at those words, fished in his jacket for his wallet, and laid two bills on the table. He dabbed at his mouth with a napkin and walked toward the door as it opened.

"Eva," he said, beaming. "How wonderful to see you again."

Before he could continue, our trio caught the mayor's eye. "My, my, my, this is a popular spot today," she said, the bright light from the plate-glass windows shining on her favorite brown pearls.

"May I buy you lunch?" Marcus asked.

"I have plans," she said, looking like a younger, haughtier version of the Queen of England. She glanced right past him. "Hello, Dub, is that gift for me?"

Marcus made a choking noise and headed out the door, looking back once more as Eva and Dub sat down at his booth and the waitress walked over to take our pie order.

"This is a thank-you gift for seeing me through my ordeal," I heard Dub say, and Eva gave a soft laugh.

———

"I'm ready to lay out those old pictures," Tammy said, sticking her head in my office.

"OK." I barely looked up from the budget numbers that plagued me. As though putting out a twice-weekly paper and trying to keep the Green school open weren't enough, I constantly found myself neck-deep in balance sheets.

"So what'd you do with them?"

"Do with what?"

"The pictures." The exasperation in her voice was a lot clearer than the numbers I examined.

"I didn't do anything with them," I said, my own tone less than jovial. "They're on your desk in the newsroom."

"That's what I thought," she said, "but they're not there anymore."

I laid my pencil down, and she looked around my office for the cardboard box. "Are you sure you didn't bring it in here?"

"Tammy, I left them right where they were. You must have overlooked them."

An hour later, with Iris and Stan joining in a building-wide search, we gave up. The photos had disappeared. "That beats anything I've ever seen," Stan said.

"They'll turn up," I said.

Tammy had left to shoot a check-passing picture at a local business by the time Linda came back from an interview. I was working in the newsroom while Linda straightened her desk. After a moment or two, a look of frustration crossed her face.

"Did you take the school file?" she asked. "I need it to wrap up this story."

"The school file?"

"The one with my background material, my interview notes, that sort of thing." She looked around. "It was lying right here."

"Are you sure?"

"Of course I'm sure. I'm the most organized person in this building."

"I suppose it's too much to hope that you have the box of reader photos," I said, a familiar sense of foreboding creeping up on me.

"Tammy had those," she said.

"I think we've been robbed," I said. "The old school pictures are missing, too."

"Robbed?" She looked around. "I'm calling Doug right now."

"I'm not sure I want to get the police chief involved yet," I said. "It'll complicate things."

"He always knows what to do," Linda said. "I could ask him as a friend."

"Give me a quick moment," I said, and jogged back to the pressroom, where Stan was up to his elbows in ink and grease, his jumpsuit covered in black gunk.

"Is there a problem with the press?" I asked, panic in my voice. "Has it been tampered with?"

"Tampered with?" Stan scooted out from the tight spot and stood, wiping his hands on one of the dozens of cotton cloths he kept nearby. "I'm doing routine maintenance. Nothing special."

"Thank heavens," I said. "It appears that someone came into the building while Tammy and I were at lunch." As I ran through the scenario, he stuck both hands in his pockets and listened intently.

"Let me call Doug," he said. "This is a matter for the police."

"Linda will," I said.

The chief himself responded to the call and treated our complaint with the seriousness of an international espionage case.

"You shouldn't leave the building unlocked," Doug said.

"We're a business," Linda said. "You want us to lock our customers out?"

"I was at my desk all day," Iris said. "I usually hear the bell when someone comes in."

"It was Marcus Hillburn," Tammy blurted. "He knew we were out of the building. He had means and motive."

"Means and motive?" Linda said. "You really are married to a lawyer, aren't you?"

I tried not to laugh.

"Well, he did," Tammy said. "I told Dr. Hillburn about those pictures when we saw him at the Cotton Boll. Then they came up missing."

"Readers sent those photos," I said. "Everyone in town knew we had them."

"Did they have value?" Doug asked.

"Only to us—and to their owners." I thought of the nice people who had dropped the pictures off or had mailed them in with sweet notes, often in old-fashioned script handwriting. "Those pictures are irreplaceable in many instances."

"How about the missing file?" Doug looked at Linda's desk with a smile. While Linda insisted the two were not dating, she turned to him frequently for advice on covering the police and court beats.

"I had most of it backed up elsewhere," she said. "But there were interview notes I didn't copy, plus Hillburn's resume, that sort of thing. Nothing too important."

"You located Hillburn's resume?" I asked.

"One of my sources at the school board found a copy," she said. "It was pretty clear from reading it that Dr. Marcus Hillburn thinks highly of himself."

"But that doesn't mean he'd burglarize the paper in the middle of the day," I said.

"Could Lee Roy have done it?" Iris asked.

"I hadn't even thought of that," I said. "But why?"

"To cause trouble," Linda said.

"My reports say he's doing well," Doug said. "He never misses work, meets with his probation officer as scheduled and seems to be turning his life around. This sounds like criminal mischief to me." He wrote in a small notebook as we talked. "Let me explore further. I'll notify you when I find something out."

In Friday afternoon's paper, we ran a front-page story about the photographs and offered a modest reward for their return.

"That's a little beneath Marcus in his fancy clothes and high-brow car," I said to Chris over supper. "It's too blatant, and what good would it do him?"

"Do you want me to speak to Rick about Lee Roy?"

"I know it can't be him. He acts so different," I said. "Why would he put his job in jeopardy?"

"Whoever did it is causing trouble," Chris said. "It reminds me of the fires, and I don't like it."

The next morning, I was the first to arrive at the paper, and a big black pickup was parked in the newspaper lot, Dub and Joe Sepulvado sitting in the cab. They got out as I parked, and Joe took off his cap and twisted it in his hands. He had almost fully recovered from his tornado injuries.

Dub pulled a cardboard box out of the back seat. "Joe found this while picking up cans. We think it's what you're looking for."

I looked in the box and saw the pictures, some covered with coffee grounds and water stains.

"They were in the trash behind the florist," Dub said.

"But I don't understand," I said. "How did they get in the trash?"

"I don't know, Miss Lois," Joe said, "but they were down the street."

"Joe, this is wonderful," I said. "We'll pay you a reward for returning them."

"A reward?" He looked confused. "For doing the right thing? That is . . ." He paused, searching for a word. "That is ridiculous."

Dub and I both laughed, an odd camaraderie suddenly between us.

"It is not ridiculous at all, Joe. These photographs are irreplaceable," I said. "You are a hero."

Joe dug in his pocket and pulled out a bandanna, wiping his face. "You and your husband are heroes, not me. You saved my life."

"That was Mannix. He's the one who found you." I still blushed when people praised us for finding Joe trapped in a shed.

"We're just glad Joe was rescued," Dub said. "And I think finding these photos may finally have convinced him to give up his can business. But he needs to ask you a favor."

"Of course," I said. "Anything."

"I know you're a busy woman, Miss Lois, but I have a need," Joe said, gripping the bandanna tightly. "I heard about your high school classes. I want to learn how to read."

"That would be our pleasure," I said. "Let's get in out of the cold and talk about it."

Fumbling with the lock, I watched Dub pick up the out-of-town papers on the steps. It felt weird, knowing that over the years he had come through these doors many more times than I had.

"You're a good newspaper publisher," he said, almost as though he could read my mind. "You were meant to own this paper."

I flipped on the lights and guided the men into my office, recalling the way Chuck had always tried to push me around, while his brother had been easier on me.

Dub pulled a check out of his shirt pocket and handed it my way. "I want to contribute to a legal fund to save the school," he said.

"But we don't have a legal fund," I said.

"I am asking the newspaper to start one."

———⚭———

Contributions to save the school arrived in each day's mail, often small amounts.

"Each of my girls graduated from Green High," one mother who was a retiree wrote. "I want part of my pension to help other children."

"The farmers out on Route 2 took up four hundred dollars," Bud said, dropping by with Anna Grace. "And the homemakers' guild came up with three hundred."

A fifth grader held a bake sale in her front yard and dropped off twenty-three dollars, and the Green Forward Group donated a thousand dollars.

"We need a good lawyer, and I recommend we bring Terrence on board again," Mayor Eva said. "He helped straighten things out after the storm, and he'll take a wise approach to this."

At the same time, the demand for help with the GED and literacy classes snowballed. Tammy wrote a column about her shame at not graduating and inspired local people, who begged her to help them get their diplomas.

"I've taken twenty calls this morning," she said the Wednesday after her story ran. "I had no idea there were so many people who slipped through the cracks."

Linda volunteered to help Joe learn to read, and the word quickly spread.

During a phone visit with my friend Marti in Ohio, I told her of the people who were calling. "Within the past week, we've had more potential students than we can handle. Plus, parents are calling for help for their children."

"Doesn't your Kids Club at church help with that?" she asked.

"Only to a degree. We've got more children there than we can deal with. They need tutoring for standardized testing, plus everyday help with homework."

The next morning she called back, almost breathless with excitement. "Gary suggested we bring a mission group to

Green over spring break. We can help with any students you have in mind."

"I don't know." I hesitated. "We're not a third-world country in need of missionaries."

"Lois Barker Craig, that's not what we're suggesting. We have a whole group of college students who want to help people in need. Why go out of the country if we can serve down in Green?"

Molly and Linda balked at the idea, but Tammy jumped on it with enthusiasm. "This may be a way to improve test scores and to free up local people to help in other areas."

Pastor Jean volunteered to let the visitors stay in the new church building. "This is exactly the kind of group it's designed for," she said. "We even have a shower."

"What if residents feel we're looking down our noses at them?" I asked. "I wouldn't want people to think more outsiders are criticizing us."

"We can't help what people think," Jean said. "But that doesn't have to stop us from offering help where we can."

"Marti and Gary have been to Green twice," Chris said. "They like the people here. They want to make a difference. Why not let them?"

Once more I knew I had to pray about this, not about Marti coming to help, but about my attitude. Then I picked up the phone and apologized for balking. "We'll be waiting for you with open arms," I said.

"I'll start signing students up now," Marti said. "We'll bring two vanloads for a week in March and help wherever it's needed. If you sweet-talk us, Gary and I might even work on your house."

Katy pouted when she learned her spring break didn't coincide with the Ohio group's visit and decided to round up her own volunteers.

"She's bringing ten students from her church in Georgia," Tammy said. "They've all signed up to tutor and to help with Kids Camp at Grace Chapel."

Molly didn't come around as easily.

"Does it bother anyone?" Molly asked one day in the newsroom.

Tammy was puzzled. "Why would it bother us?"

"I don't know . . . I don't want people to think that Green is dumb," Molly said.

"We have lots of smart people here, like Dr. Kevin and Lois and Coach Chris . . ."

Tammy looked hurt. "But not me?"

"You're one of the smartest people I know," Molly said. "You can do anything. But some people might be embarrassed with all of this out-of-town help."

"Is your mother embarrassed to be working on her GED?" Tammy asked, staring Molly right in the eye with a look she often used on me.

"No way," Molly said. "She's like a new person. You've helped her see all sorts of possibilities, and her boss is talking to her about a promotion."

"Maybe there's your answer," Tammy said.

Later I overheard Molly talking to Katy on the phone in the newsroom. It was hard not to eavesdrop, and, even though I had capitulated, I shared a few of her thoughts about the visitors. It was hard to swallow my pride and accept their help.

"I can't believe I was such a jerk," Molly said in a hushed voice. "I hurt Tammy's feelings because I was too proud to admit she was right."

14

When none of Sherry Berry's second-grade class showed up for school Monday, Sherry called the parents one by one. Apparently each of the students had an allergic reaction to the temporary unicorn tattoos given out at a birthday party over the weekend. Most of my neighbors didn't think the tattoos were appropriate in the first place.

—The Green News-Item

When Terrence D'Arbonne got involved in Green's case, my hope grew that things might turn out better—for the school and for my friend Kevin's love life.

Even if he couldn't keep the school open, I still wanted Kevin to fall head-over-heels in love with him.

Mayor Eva had complete confidence in the attorney, and, over lunch at the country club, told me her plans. "He's got the best legal mind I've ever known," she said. "He's one of those rare people who can see the big picture and handle logistics."

"He's cute, too," I said, trying to make her smile. Always a serious woman, she had been especially somber since Marcus had appeared in Green. "I wish Kevin would trust him."

Eva was not one for what I considered girl talk, but she didn't change the subject. "I thought they had been dating for a few months," she said.

"They get together when they can," I said, "but between her medical practice and Asa and Terrence's work and the drive between here and Alexandria . . . It's tough."

The mayor nodded. "If it's supposed to work out, it will. I learned a long time ago that you can't force something like that."

"Something like that? Are you talking about love, Eva?"

She picked up a file folder and held it almost like a shield between us. "I suppose I am. I know you will keep this in the highest confidence, but it's shaken me to see Marcus after all these years. I suppose no one likes being reminded of their mistakes."

"He's a good-looking man," I said. "A smooth talker, too."

"I fell for him hook, line, and sinker. We had the big society wedding at the Presbyterian church downtown. Had the reception in this very room, although the décor was more traditional. I thought I had the world in the palm of my hand."

Thinking about her celebrating in this very room, I stopped eating.

"I was a young woman with stars in my eyes," she said. "Thank goodness I got past that."

"Did you come back to Green immediately after Marcus . . . left?"

She nodded. "I tucked my tail between my legs and ran home to Mama and Daddy and my big brother. Major looked out for me in those days, and he hated Marc. I suspect he still does. I figured Marc would be the one to wind up in jail, not my brother."

"Why would you think such a thing?"

"Even in those days, my ex was always wheeling and dealing," she said. "Looking back, he loved my family money and Daddy's influence with the college president more than he loved me."

"It's a good thing for Green that you didn't stay in Texas," I said. "You hold this town together. I've never known a leader like you." I grinned. "I want to be like you when I grow up."

Eva laughed. "You balance love and work better than I ever did. I've hidden behind business and politics for years. Those can be messy, but they don't eat at your heart. Plus, there's always another challenge to face, like this school crisis."

"What does Dub think about all this?" I asked.

"He sees Marc as a threat, to me and to Green. He'd rather I not have anything to do with him."

"So he's jealous?"

"'Apprehensive' would be a better word. Dub and I hardly spoke for years, as you well know. I made poor choices, and so did he. We're not to the jealous stage yet."

"I must disagree. That man is well past the jealous stage. He loves you," I said. "He certainly wants what's best for you. It's terribly sweet, actually."

"That may be the nicest thing you've ever said about him," she said with a small smile.

"I find it easier to let him off the hook because he's so good to you."

"I like that about you, Lois. You deal with something and let it go."

"Me?" I stopped. "I can hold onto a grudge longer than anyone, even Tammy."

"I heard Lee Roy Hicks is working at your house," she said. "That doesn't sound like holding a grudge to me."

"He goes by Lee now," I said. "He's trying to change. I used to be afraid of him, but I've learned a lot about second chances since I moved here." I shrugged. "Chris and I are trying to forgive him."

"Sounds a little like me and Dub," she said. "I look back and feel like I handled this all wrong thirty years ago. I never should have chosen Marc over Dub."

"It's never too late to make things right," I said, hearing the voice of the late Aunt Helen, my friend and mentor when I moved to Green. "We can't live in the past, no matter how strong it pulls. We have to move forward."

"I'll give that some thought," Eva said with the tiniest of smiles. "It's a lot easier to run the town than my own life."

"That's why people say I'm bossy," I said, cutting a piece of cheesecake to share with her. "I'd rather tell you what to do than have to figure out my own stuff."

By the time the valet brought our cars around, I felt as though momentous events had been set in motion.

Terrence would be in and out of Green frequently, and Kevin would be unable to resist him this time.

Eva would allow her controlled, organized, focused heart to fall in love with the man she had loved since he was a boy.

Who knew what would develop from the visit, but the mayor let me buy our lunch, so I planned to take credit if everything worked out.

Talking with Eva about her love life was a milestone in our friendship. Finding myself in a conversation with Dub about it was a total shock.

He was working in the flower bed at Maria's mobile home one Saturday afternoon when I stopped by with a box of groceries from the church. Maria's three sons were out back in the garden with Joe Sepulvado. From where I stood, it looked like Joe was tilling, and the boys were having a dirt-clod fight.

"Maria had to work today," Dub said, taking the food from my small trunk. "Joe's keeping the children, and I'm getting that bed ready for spring."

"You two really help out around here," I said. "Her deck looks great, and those new trees seem to be making it through winter fine."

"It's nothing." He set the box on the porch. "They're a fine family, and it helps me more than it does them. It's a good diversion for Joe, too. His wife's been gone for nearly a year now, and he hasn't seen his children and grandchildren in Mexico in nearly three years."

I looked around the place, Chris's former trailer, now settled on the new lot, looking as though it had been there forever. "It looks so homey," I said. "I'll be glad when our house gets back in shape."

"How's the remodeling coming?" Dub asked.

I wrinkled my face. "It's coming together slowly."

"I renovated a home years ago. It was one of the most awful experiences of my life. That's about the time I decided that building new subdivisions would be a better idea."

"Your development on the lake is beautiful, but I love Route 2. We'll have a great house one of these days." I gestured at the flower bed. "I can't wait to get the yard fixed up. Your Aunt Helen had done such a good job with it, but between the storm and the construction, it's a mess."

He nodded. "I'll be happy to help you and Chris when you get ready. Joe's probably up for that, too. We're always looking for something to do."

"You mean that, don't you?" I said with a small frown. "You really want to help people."

He picked up a rake and spread pine bark at the base of the small plants. "I wasted too many years and let a lot of bad things happen—did a few of them myself. I'm trying to make up for lost time."

"Does that include your relationship with Eva?" I asked, wishing I could pull the words back as soon as they were spoken.

"You always did cut to the chase," he said, bending down to pack the mulch with his hand.

"Chris would say it's not any of my business, but I think highly of the mayor." I could feel my face flushing.

"You've been good for Eva," he said. "She's a true public servant, and you've helped her see why that matters. If we can get through this school situation, maybe things will settle down for a while."

"Your donation to the legal fund has been a big help," I said. "I'd have never thought of that if you hadn't brought it up."

"You would have, sooner or later," he said. "Lawyers don't come cheap, and we need a good lawyer to win this one. All we have to do is outlast Marcus Hillburn."

"Outlast him?"

"Men like that hit and run," he said. "This is his project du jour, but he won't stick with it for the long haul. If he can't settle this quickly, he'll move on to another client. I've seen it happen time and again."

"He's pretty slick."

"Just because a man roars into town in a fancy car, dressed in expensive clothes, doesn't mean he's smart."

"He gets under your skin in a big way, doesn't he?"

"Lois, I got arrested for illegal practices, covered up my brother's sins for years, and let the woman I love push me away for more than half my life. The most important thing to me now is to do right by Eva."

An almost mischievous smile appeared, and I saw a glimpse of what Eva found appealing. "That man makes me feel like I am ten again and need to fight someone on the playground," Dub said. "He annoys me, pure and simple."

He raked a minute more. The only sounds to be heard were Maria's boys playing out back and a crow cawing overhead. Dub's voice was gruff, almost as though he were choked up, when he spoke again.

"I won't let Marcus—or anyone else—draw me off course from doing what's right. I am through living like that. I don't understand it, but I believe God sent Eva and Joe—and even you, as strange as it sounds—to help me be the man I was meant to be all along, not the one I had become."

He leaned against the rake. "I sure don't deserve it, but I'm mighty thankful."

15

Have you seen Yvonne Matheny's deviled-egg dish? She says she left it at someone's house after a funeral, and it hasn't been returned. "My bunco group asked me to bring my special eggs to our monthly birthday meeting, and I don't know how to haul them without that tray. It was my great-aunt Johnnie's, and I hope it turns up."

—The Green News-Item

Eugene Ellis placed the call for an appointment at the newspaper, clerical duties now apparently part of his job.

"Miss Robinson would like to clear up a few things," he said. "She believes she is being unfairly criticized for doing her job."

"I'll be happy to hear what she has to say," I said, although I had heard plenty. "If you don't mind, I'll ask Terrence and Eva and my staff to sit in."

"I'll give her the message." He sighed heavily.

"Eugene?" I asked before he hung up. "Chris and I are worried about you."

"No need to be," he said. "I've been through ups and downs at the school for forty-some-odd years. I'll see you next week."

Priscilla and Eugene gathered in the *Item* parking lot with an entourage, including Katy's father and his assistant superintendent and two school board members. I hadn't seen a group like this descend on a paper since a congressional race in Dayton. The mayor and Terrence had arrived earlier and were seated in the conference room with Linda. The sides had shaped up in this skirmish.

"Dr. Hillburn will join us shortly," Priscilla said. "He was unavoidably delayed in traffic."

"He should have left earlier, if you ask me," Tammy said, ushering the principal in and taking a seat at the table.

The principal scowled and directed each of her group to their chairs, like an elementary teacher getting her pupils lined up. When Eugene chose a place near Eva, Priscilla made a noise that sounded like a snort and pointed to the chair next to her.

Eugene moved further away.

Before I could welcome the group, Priscilla stood up, both hands flat on the table. Her blonde hair was arranged so that it dipped in front of her shoulders, and, up close, her makeup seemed too heavy.

She looked around the room, accusation in her eyes. "I want to talk about the truth," she proclaimed.

"Then it sounds like we want the same thing," Mayor Eva said.

"This is a complex issue that must be handled profession-ally," the younger woman said.

"Why were we not given more notice to clear this up?" Terrence said, standing and putting his hands on the table in the same pose Priscilla had struck.

The principal gritted her teeth. "My prepared comments clear up many misunderstandings." She paused, as though daring anyone to interrupt. "If I may?"

Terrence looked at me and the mayor and sat back down.

"The state controls funding," Priscilla said. "Accusations of misspending fly around this town, but the superintendent can tell you we can't spend money we don't have."

James seemed to ponder whether to speak. "We've been cut, and we've been cut deep," he said firmly. "The state says shut small schools down, or step aside and let them do it. We don't get the support for education we once had."

The other school board member, an African American store owner, spoke next. "My job is to do what voters want, but how can I do that if we don't have the resources to pay for it?"

"Louisiana has always paid a large share of our school budget," a school board member, a woman a few years older than I, said. "When they up and stopped paying, we didn't have any choice. It's like when my brother-in-law quit paying his child support. My sister lost her house."

"Furthermore," Priscilla continued, as though no one had spoken, "this is a fluid situation."

"Excuse me," Terrence said, standing again. "As the legal representative for Green, I must clarify a few things before we move on. My clients are unclear about whether the plans to close the school are legally binding. Confusion abounds on why you are taking the lead on this issue, when the responsibility rests with the superintendent and school board?"

"Mr. D'Arbonne," the school board member practically wailed, "we didn't have a choice."

"We didn't have much choice," Eugene said and stood slowly, assuming what had become the popular hands-on-table stance. "I thought I could sit this one out. I'm close to retirement and didn't want to rock the boat. But everyone has lost sight of what matters most—whether our children can read and write, how we're going to help them graduate and find jobs. When it comes to those issues, there's always a choice."

"Mr. Ellis," Priscilla said in a stern tone, "take your seat, and let us continue."

"Ma'am, I'm afraid I can't do that," he said and turned to the superintendent. "James, you and me go way back. You're a good man, and I know you would never intentionally hurt students. But we have let ourselves be steamrolled by Baton Rouge."

Katy's father grew still.

"In the end, we may not be able to keep a school in Green," Eugene continued. "But we have choices. We could have four-day school, like they're doing in some places. We could trim positions, at the school and parish level. We could use the expertise of people like Miss Robinson here to find ways to improve the school rather than close it."

"Eugene, I don't like it any more than you do," James said, "but it is inevitable that Green High will close. Every small town in the country faces this. We're no different."

"Could we be?" Eugene asked. "What if we use the time and energy we're spending to come up with a plan? I'm not talking about a pie-in-the-sky plan, but a realistic approach."

Mayor Eva stood, and I was relieved when she didn't lean over the table. "We owe it to the students to try harder."

"What's going on here, Eva?" Marcus asked, striding through the door with his leather briefcase, Molly behind him, her overloaded backpack slung over her shoulder.

"I hope I didn't miss too much," Molly said. "I had class."

"I was detoured around roadwork," Marcus said. "My GPS neglected to notify me that there would be a major shift in the route I was taking."

"Thank goodness you've arrived," Priscilla said, ignoring Molly and walking over to Marcus, putting her hand on his sleeve, looking more like his girlfriend than his colleague. "I've been unable to make my point with this group. They don't understand economic imperatives."

"Miss Robinson, I was working on economic imperatives before you were born," Eugene said. "You want to talk about truth here today. The truth is we will have a hard time coming up with money. The truth is that Green students tend to be poor and don't test well. The truth is that they need more help with school, not less."

James cleared his throat and squirmed. "Eugene, we all are torn up over this, but we can't change directions in a heartbeat."

Eugene stood and faced him, an unspoken message flowing between them.

Priscilla's face grew red, and she stood, opening her mouth but then closing it without saying anything. Marcus seemed to be trying to figure out what was happening.

"What do you suggest we do?" James asked, looking around the room.

"We make ourselves heard, starting with the facts in this case," Eva said. "We ask each of you to fight for us, not against us."

"We want collaboration and cooperation, just as you do," Priscilla said, sounding like a mass-mailed human resources brochure.

"No, you don't," Eva said. The two powerful women stared at each other. "You want to win."

"So do you," Priscilla said.

Eva almost looked surprised. "We're quite a bit alike, aren't we? I have been known to yield from time to time, but not when something matters this much."

"Is this meeting going somewhere?" Marcus asked.

"I can't speak for the meeting, but I'm going somewhere," Eugene said. He moved toward the door but stopped.

"I've invested my life in this school and the education of this community," he said. "I'm not as young as I used to be, and I had hoped to wrap up my career a little easier than this. But I'm going to walk to Baton Rouge with Molly."

The college student's gasp was the first of several. "That's great," she said with a dazzling smile.

"Of all the ridiculous . . ." Priscilla swept her notes into her satchel and picked up her small purse. "Eugene, if you're not back at the school within the hour, you're fired."

"You can't fire him," James said.

Terrence, all business, crossed his arms. "Ladies and gentlemen," he said, "might I suggest we reconvene after a brief break?"

"As far as the school system goes, there's nothing further to discuss," Marcus said. "I've seen far larger—and smarter— schools lose this battle."

"But, Marc, my dear," the mayor said, "you've never seen Green in action."

Linda intercepted the consultant on his way out of the building. "Mr. Hillburn, I'd like a word with you. I'm working on a story that only you can address."

"It's Dr. Hillburn," he said and paused, as though torn between pontificating and wanting to distance himself from the little people for whom he had so little regard.

"Marcus," Priscilla said. "We need to regroup before we make any statements to the media." Her voice lowered. "We'll do better with the television stations in Shreveport, so our comments aren't taken out of context."

"This won't take more than a few minutes," Linda said, waving several sheets of cream-colored paper in the air. "I want to go over Mr. Hillburn's resume."

———⌀———

The next few days were filled with renewed attention to school coverage, and the twice-weekly editions and website overflowed with questions and comments. I wrote another front-page column asking for everyone to let us know what they thought Green should do, and we published an in-depth Q&A with James, who explained challenges and possibilities.

Marcus was still trying to explain why he claimed a PhD he didn't actually have, a scandal Linda had unearthed. Eugene Ellis was working with the school system to take a leave of absence to walk to Baton Rouge with his former student and a newspaper photographer.

Chris had overheard Priscilla trying to reach the governor on the phone and slamming the receiver down when she couldn't get through.

"How'd you know that Marcus lied about his credentials?" Tammy asked Linda during one of our afternoon visits in the newsroom.

"From you," Linda said, hunched over her computer as usual. "When you confessed to misleading us about your high school diploma, I started wondering about other people. Unfortunately for Marcus, his name was the first to pop into my mind. To be fair, I investigated Lois, too. You made good grades."

"And they say your college transcript doesn't matter," I said. "Only a great reporter makes those kinds of connections, Linda. You're a natural at this."

"I learned it from y'all," she said. "Now if you two would leave me alone, I'm nailing down this gap in Miss Priscilla Robinson's work history and trying to figure out how long she and Marcus dated when she was in Texas."

Molly and Tammy fretted over how to involve more of the community in the walk to Baton Rouge.

"Everyone is so quick to throw out ideas and criticize our town," Molly said. "They talk and talk, but they need to do more."

"Walk the walk," Tammy said, clapping her hands together. "Let's have a community walk. They have them up in Shreveport all the time."

Molly's eyes sparkled. "We can ask people not only to talk the talk but walk the walk. We can have T-shirts and facts on getting a GED and that sort of thing."

"We need sponsors," Linda said. "Katy's great at this kind of thing. We can ask her to set up a campaign online. Is that OK, Lois?"

I drew a deep breath. "Isn't everyone stretched a little thin for all this?"

"Are you kidding?" Tammy said. "We're just getting warmed up."

Within three weeks, the pair had pulled together a communitywide event, dragging in everyone they came in contact with. Eva's department store donated money for "Walk the Walk" T-shirts, with the slogan written in white on a green chalkboard. The Cotton Boll Café agreed to set up a water station, and the local radio station offered to play music from a live broadcast.

"There's not that much that happens in Green on Saturday mornings," Molly said. "People are happy to help. Katy's even coming home for it."

"Spring's on its way, and everyone's tired of being cooped up," Tammy said. "We have a hundred walkers signed up, and more will show up that morning."

In keeping with the area's unpredictable weather, a cold front moved in the day before the walk, nipping back fresh buds on plants and bringing out an assortment of sweatshirts, gloves, and knit caps for the event.

"Now I have to figure out how to get the group portrait with the matching shirts," Tammy said. "It was going to look so good."

Several of us gathered on Friday afternoon to sort shirts and put together packets. Molly had taken Anthony for a follow-up visit with a doctor in Shreveport, but Katy had made it in early.

"The teacher doesn't make us show up on Fridays," she said, "if we don't want to."

"Why is it that students don't worry about getting their money's worth out of tuition?" I asked.

She started to argue and then laughed. "You're probably right."

"You've sure been home a lot lately," Tammy said. "It's fun having you here, but you're not having trouble at school, are you?"

"I guess I'm a little homesick," she admitted, "and things are hard for my parents right now—with all the school stuff. It takes their minds off it when I come home."

"Your stepdad's job is harder than running a newspaper," I said.

"That's what he says." Katy folded another shirt. "It's easy to say 'keep the school open,' but it's hard to pay for it. We don't have as many kids as we used to."

By the time Molly arrived, we had the plastic sacks neatly arranged in alphabetical order, ready for participants to pick them up in the lobby, and Katy had started on posters. The two girls hugged, Katy squealed, and then she grabbed her friend's hands.

"How's Anthony?" she asked.

"He's better, but it's a lot harder than I thought it would be. I hoped he'd be walking by now."

With all the school hassles, I sometimes forgot to ask her about her boyfriend. "Things take time," I said.

"I used to think that sounded lame," Katy said, "but it's the truth."

"He's getting discouraged," Molly said. "His mother needs help around the house, and he worries that he won't be able to go to college next year. He was counting on a basketball scholarship, and nobody's interested in a guy who can't walk."

———— ❦ ————

Iris arrived early Saturday to set up tables with brochures about the GED and other community courses. Anthony's mother volunteered to help with the displays, and Molly's mother changed her work shift to sign latecomers in.

Chris and Stan had mapped the 3.1-mile course through downtown, marking a one-mile "fun run" for those who weren't up to the 5K. Pastor Jean, her husband, and the Methodist preacher were stationed along the path to make sure participants didn't make a wrong turn.

Daylight had barely broken when Joe Sepulvado and Dub showed up, ready to help. "Put us to work," Dub said, and the two roped off a chute near the finish line and set up a few metal chairs for onlookers.

Maria and her sons came closer to race time, and the boys ran to Joe, showing off new tennis shoes, a broad smile on everyone's faces.

"I think Maria's sweet on Joe," Tammy said, twirling her hair around her finger. "I wonder if anything will ever come of that."

"I must be losing my matchmaking abilities," I said. "I hadn't even noticed, and I can't get Terrence and Kevin together."

"Be patient," Tammy said. "Remember it took you a while to fall in love with Chris."

Our talk was interrupted by Molly, who insisted I officially welcome participants, handing me a bullhorn Linda had borrowed from the police department and a bell from Rose's antique mall. I was walking to the starting spot when I saw Priscilla standing to the side, wearing a pair of black slacks and a black silk shirt.

"What are you doing here?" I snapped. "Isn't it a little early to celebrate the death of the school?"

She stared at me. "You have everything all figured out, don't you? It must be nice to be right about everything."

"I understand this community," I said.

"Because you lucked into owning a newspaper and marrying the town's most eligible bachelor?"

Ouch. "At least I didn't come into town to destroy something," I said, noticing people lining up for the walk out of the corner of my eye.

She shook her head, and a glimmer of doubt showed on her face. I couldn't tell if it was aimed at my motives or her own.

"I'm the principal of the school," she said. "Despite what you believe, I came today to indicate my support of public schools."

"Don't you mean your support of closing public schools?"

"Everything isn't as simple as you make it out to be," she said and walked off, stiff and alone in the midst of the crowd.

My conscience was cloudy as I started the race.

Molly stood behind Anthony's wheelchair at the front, and Katy pushed Adam, Anthony's brother, in a stroller. Iris Jo held his little sister's hand, and his mother stood nearby. Eva walked over from near her store, wearing a navy blue jogging suit and smiling as she made eye contact with Dub.

I lifted the bullhorn to my mouth and clanged the bell. "On your mark, get set, go."

16

Lurain Henry is going through photos, bulletins and scrapbooks at the old Parkview Baptist Chapel as it prepares to be sold. If you'd like to run by and take a look, let Miss Lurain know, but she says she can't allow you to take items off the premises.

—*The Green News-Item*

The last workman was pulling out when I got in from work on Friday evening. Chris and Rick were sprawled at the kitchen table, the builder's ever-present clipboard sitting next to them.

"I'm getting an update," Chris said, standing. "Want to join us?"

"Any news?" I looked at Rick.

"A little behind schedule and a little over budget," he said with a smile. "The bedrooms and sunroom have been taped and floated and textured. The baseboards and the rest of the molding have been stripped and stained and can be installed soon."

He looked at his list. "The extra electrical outlets have been placed and the wiring's all set. The painter may be able to start in a week or so. Have you decided on your colors yet?"

"That's Lois's department," Chris said. "All I ask is that the paint matches my catfish collection."

"I thought that blew away," Rick said.

"No such luck," I said. "It's safely ensconced in the attic at Hugh and Estelle's. What can you suggest in a delicate camouflage tone?"

Despite the joking and progress on the house, I couldn't quite commit to choices. The plastic box piled high with magazines and catalogues sat in the corner of our bedroom/den, and the loose-leaf binder of decorating ideas and notes was worn from my constant scrutiny, but I balked at wrapping things up.

At our Friday night dinner at Brocato's Marina Inn on the lake, Chris asked me about appliances for the kitchen and mentioned furniture shopping in Shreveport. "What if we make a weekend of it sometime?"

"Sounds fun," I said. "But I don't see how we can go until after school's out."

He frowned. "That's more than three months away."

"The house won't be finished for months. You know that."

"I thought you'd like to get ideas and get started on the kitchen."

"You heard Rick," I said. "It'll be months before we're ready to move in."

"Move in? We live there already."

"Not really," I said. "Oh, look—is that Kevin and Terrence coming in? I wonder if they'd like to join us, or if they want to be alone?"

"This reminds me of looking at houses," he said. "You're trying to get off this topic."

"We hardly ever get to visit with Kevin." I gave my best innocent smile.

He squeezed my hand affectionately. "I'll ask them."

The couple was dressed as though visiting a five-star restaurant in a city, Kevin beautiful as always in knee-length skirt and cropped blazer. Terrence had on a sports jacket over a nice golf shirt. I glanced down at my jeans and striped oxford shirt and wondered why I hadn't gone to more trouble for my date with my husband.

"I didn't know you two were going out tonight." I made no effort to hide my delight.

Kevin put a big teasing look on her face. "Did my receptionist forget to send you my calendar again?"

"I was in town for a school meeting," Terrence said. "I begged Kevin to let me take her to dinner."

"We heard crawfish are already in season," Kevin said. "I nearly had to tackle Terrence to get him to come here instead of that roadside stand out by the interstate."

"It was this or PB&J for Chris," I said with a grimace. "Not much of a choice."

The dinner conversation quickly shifted to our house project, which was a close second to Green schools in what everyone talked about.

"Stop by sometime," Chris said. "It's coming along great."

"It's a little behind schedule," I said. "But it looks good."

Kevin threw out a few ideas from her own experience in fixing up a cluster of houses, including her own, in the Lakeside neighborhood. "Stay simple," she said. "Rick's a great builder, but everyone has an idea what you ought to do, and it all costs extra."

"Tell me about it," Chris said.

As we walked to our cars after a delicious meal, Kevin fell behind while Terrence and Chris talked about spring training for baseball. "You don't seem quite like yourself tonight," she said. "What's wrong?"

"Remodeling," I said. "I don't know how you've fixed up all of those places."

"I wasn't living in them at the time," she said. "All that dust gets old."

"I find myself longing for your parents' motel. Maybe we should have stayed there."

"Oh, Lois." Kevin touched my shoulder. "Your home is going to be wonderful."

"I hope so." I slowed my steps. "How are things with you and Terrence?"

"About like you and your house," she said. "He's a nice guy, but I'm not ready to get serious."

"Give him a chance," I whispered. "He's perfect for you."

"And your house is perfect for you."

———

"Dad, can Lois and I use the four-wheeler?" Chris asked after our Saturday morning breakfast the next day.

"Be sure to show her those things in the little house," Estelle said before Hugh could reply.

"I need to get to work," I said. "You go on without me."

"No way." He pulled me to my feet and steered me toward the back door. "It's too pretty a day to stay inside. Besides, my father found some things he thinks you may like for the house."

Until coming to Green, I'd not seen a four-wheeler up close and never dreamed about riding on one. For Chris, taking a spin was a favorite way to unwind, roaming around his parents' land, the dogs running alongside barking and wrestling. I usually chatted with my mother-in-law while he rode or went into the newspaper office for my Saturday morning catch-up chores.

"Why not? Let me help your mama clean up, and I'll be right there."

My sisters-in-law, each married to Craig brothers, stood. "It's our turn," one said. "No dishes for you today."

"Go have fun," his younger brother said. "We'll keep an eye on that fur ball of yours."

Holly Beth barked, as though knowing he was talking about her.

While I had longed for years to get married, I had not realized how many different ways it would enrich me. Being part of the Craig family was so comfortable and brought a whole new level of love to my life. When I walked into their home, it was as though both of us—not just Chris—had come home.

Holding hands, we walked out to the metal carport, where the four-wheeler sat among a variety of tools and equipment, and Chris attached the little garden wagon. "In case those house things are half as good as Daddy thinks they are," he said, lifting me onto the four-wheeler seat. "Let's ride a while and take a look."

Like many rural North Louisiana residents, the Craigs had an assortment of out-buildings, filled with everything from hay to rusty farm tools. Anything someone didn't need but couldn't bear to throw away was stashed in one of the buildings and seldom seen again.

Chris and I rode along a dirt trail that wound behind the house and up past Hugh's beloved chicken coop. An ancient structure known in the family as the little house, where Estelle's mother and father had once lived, sat a few hundred yards from the Craig home, with a tin shed next to it. On the other side of the land was a small barn with a corral and a couple of horses.

Settling with my arms around my husband, I soaked up the feeling of the pre-spring day and put my worries about work aside. We bounced along the trail, and I held on tight, loving Chris.

Mannix, Markey, and Kramer ran wild, chasing invisible animals and rolling in the brown grass. Occasionally my husband pointed to a bird or a tree covered with buds.

Riding along the fence line, we stopped suddenly, and Chris turned his body and gave me a big kiss. "I think we're actually having a normal day," he said. "No community gatherings, no fights with school administrators, no home-repair projects. This feels great."

"I didn't realize how much I needed a break," I said. "What a beautiful spot."

We climbed off the four-wheeler, and Chris threw sticks for the dogs while I looked for wild flowers, a sure sign spring was headed our way. "Thanks for getting me outdoors," I said. "I get so wrapped up in work that I miss things like this."

After another few minutes riding around the farm, we pulled up at the little house. "You don't think there are rats in there, do you?" I asked.

"Maybe mice."

I shuddered. "You told me nothing decent ever got stored out here. Perhaps we ought to take a pass on this." I pulled on the sleeve of his shirt. "Look at those yellow flowers."

"Nice try, but I'm going in," he said. "You aren't going to let a few mice keep you from exploring, are you?"

"When you put it like that . . ." I stood back as he shoved the sagging door open. A shaft of light shone through a hole in the roof, making his brown hair gleam. A bird fussed at us from a branch in what had once been the front yard.

Stepping through the door, I smelled mold and mildew and saw boxes and furniture stacked everywhere. Suddenly tears started down my cheeks. As I tried to dash them away, Chris turned around, exclaimed, and hurried toward me. "Did you get stung?"

I shook my head and nestled up against him. "I still can't believe it."

"What's wrong?"

"I can't believe that a place like this is still here, and Aunt Helen's house was blown way. It catches me by surprise."

"I know, honey." He caressed my hair. "I miss that house, too. I was looking forward to living there with you."

"I'm sorry for crying on our beautiful morning. I don't know what came over me."

"You've been so busy you haven't taken a second to relax. You're sad—for the house and your friend Tom and everything that vanished. That doesn't go away overnight."

"You always know what to say." I gave him a small smile. "Let's go inside."

Standing back, I watched Chris dig through boxes and piles of old stuff, ranging from an old metal bucket with a laundry detergent logo to a wooden spice rack with dirty white jars.

When he opened the top drawer of a rickety chest of drawers, a mouse jumped out and scurried off. I screamed and turned to run, but then my eye caught a rainbow reflecting from a prism.

"Oh, Chris, look. It's a chandelier."

"Let there be light," he said and carefully pulled the fixture from a near-shredded blanket. "Look, here's something else." He pulled out two white ceramic sconces, painted with flowers, and a white lamp with a dogwood painted on it. "This one is a little cracked."

I studied it. "That's not too bad."

We dug through a few more boxes and a water-stained wooden trunk and found a tiny porcelain sink, a medicine chest made of beaded board, and a thermometer advertising root beer. In a corner, I discovered a massive green shutter. "This would make a great headboard for our bed," I said.

Judy Christie

"I'm beginning to think I should have brought the truck," Chris said, rearranging our load in the little wagon.

"I can't believe you haven't brought me out here before," I said, hauling the base of a concrete birdbath from the edge of the shed.

"As I recall, you said you and rats didn't get along, and you'd rather not."

"I didn't think there was anything good out here."

"I guess that depends on your definition of the word 'good.'" He helped me onto the four-wheeler. "I think most of these were at Grandma Craig's house originally."

Suddenly a weight I had not even realized I'd been carrying lifted from my shoulders. "You mean our house?" I asked, and snuggled up against him for the ride back.

———

The big old Craig place that we were remodeling had drawn me to it from the first time I laid eyes on it.

When Chris surprised me by moving the house onto the lot where my cottage had stood, a big chunk of my heart was repaired.

Today, when we turned into our driveway, the sun glowed through bare branches and new, light-green leaves. The yard didn't look so muddy. I could see the first hint of life on the pink dogwood tree in the front yard.

Dub's black truck was backed into the yard, with a couple of vehicles I didn't recognize on the side of the road. Joe shoveled dirt from the bed of the truck onto the yard, and Dub was spreading it.

Maria raked leaves that had accumulated over the winter, and her two younger boys pretended to fly, occasionally crash-landing into the piles their mother had carefully made, while the oldest boy sat on the steps with a book.

"What in the world?" I asked, trying to calm Holly Beth, who had started jumping around when she saw the guests. The other three dogs leapt from the truck as soon as it stopped, and Mannix made a beeline to Joe, who took his head in both his hands and let Mannix lick his face.

"Looks like a garden party," Chris said.

A movement in the side yard caught my attention, and I saw Lee Roy wrestle with a post on a birdhouse. As we got out of the truck, he laid it down and walked over to Chris. He avoided me when possible, showing no ill feelings but seeming to think I wouldn't want him near.

"I hope this is OK," he said. "Your friends wanted to help with your yard, and I thought I could put this purple martin house up."

Maria and the others walked over as I inspected the big white birdhouse. With its green roof, it looked like a miniature version of our house.

"That's amazing," I said. "Did you make that, Joe?" The Mexican farmer had turned out to be a first-rate handyman and had mentioned learning to read woodcraft books.

"Oh, no, ma'am," Joe said. "Mr. Hicks did that. He's got a real talent for woodworking."

The other man flushed. "I had a few months to practice," Lee Roy said with a mocking laugh. "It was either these or license plates."

Chris reached out and shook his hand. "Thanks, man," he said. "I think I prefer birdhouses."

"You may not attract any martins this year," Lee Roy said, "but they can sure help with your mosquito problem."

"Thank you," I said, placing my hand on his arm. "That is a wonderful gift."

"Lee makes bluebird houses, too," Maria's oldest son said. He had walked over from the steps and held a book on attracting

193

backyard birds. "He loaned me this book so I can build one. Mr. Dub says our yard is the kind of place bluebirds like."

"Lois mentioned needing some yard work done," Dub said to Chris, "and I had this dirt left from a load we had hauled in." He seemed embarrassed. "We're getting your yard ready for spring."

"Many thanks," Chris said, and I remembered how Dub had mowed my yard when I hardly knew him, not even mentioning the good deed.

"What a thoughtful thing to do," I said and gave Dub a hug that seemed as ordinary as one I might give Eva or Tammy or any number of friends.

"What's all that?" the youngest of Maria's sons asked, pointing at Chris's overloaded pickup. Everyone looked at the pile of stuff we had scavenged, as though eager to hear the answer.

Chris laughed and rubbed the boy's hair. "Lois found a few things at my parents' house," he said.

"In the trash?" Joe asked, his eyes wide.

"Something like that," I said, smiling. "Are you all ready for lunch?"

For the next few hours, the big scarred house looked like a scene in a movie. Maria and I sat on the swing Chris had bought for the yard, and the men and boys sat on the tailgate of the truck and the steps, passing a giant bag of potato chips back and forth and polishing off a tin of brownies Estelle had sent home with us.

Later the boys threw a Frisbee to the dogs, who, all except for Mannix, chased it until they were panting. The three-legged dog never got more than a few feet from Mr. Sepulvado, who chatted in Spanish with Maria and Dub.

The latter occasionally held up a hand to ask them to slow down. "Whoa," he said, laughing. "I'm new at this."

Lee Roy and Chris finished putting up the martin house, setting it in concrete, and I trimmed bushes and pulled up stubborn vines, wearing a pair of leather garden gloves Dub had pulled out of a toolbox in his truck.

"This is a fine place you have here," he said when he handed the gloves to me. "Aunt Helen would love what you're doing."

"I wish she could see it," I said softly.

"Me, too," he said, removing his sunglasses and wiping his eyes.

The air was cool, but not cold, and the scent of a small clump of old jonquils meandered through the air by the front porch.

When everyone drove off, Chris and I wandered through the house and talked about the next projects.

"The bathrooms are nearly finished," he said. "What color is that tile again? Mississippi Mud?" He squeezed my hand.

"Tundra taupe," I said with a smile. "I'm glad you insisted on white fixtures. They look perfect with the chrome."

"The old trim looks great," he said. "I'm glad we stained it instead of painting."

"All your idea, and you know it." I pulled out a paint chip. "This cream color will look great with that light fixture we found. And this yellow will brighten up the kitchen."

Steadily, I updated our project calendar. "We've made more progress than I realized," I said. "It's almost time to start on the kitchen and the living room."

My heart swelled, and I took Chris by the hand. "Let's look at everything again."

I had wept that morning, exploring a shack that had lasted for decades. I had laughed this afternoon, working in the yard with the oddest assortment of new friends.

Now, after months of struggle, I let myself fall in love with our home.

17

Bud Johnson reports the first sighting of ripening dew-berries. The Natchitoches Parish farmer spotted several patches of berries near stands of willow on the Red River, where vines grow wild on the river bank. Extension Service agent Martha Martin says it takes a quart of dewberries to make a good cobbler. "There's nothing better for Sunday morning breakfast," says Johnson, "than a handful of berries and a plateful of catfish."

—The Green News-Item

The vanloads of Ohio students rolled into Green one week before my first wedding anniversary and a few hours after our church service.

Marti jumped out first, nearly knocking me to the ground in the new Grace Chapel parking lot.

"It looks so different," she said, gesturing at the church. "But you look the same."

Gary followed her down the steps and shook hands with Chris. "Look at our handsome husbands," Marti said. "I can't believe we're married."

The stream of students, some from college and some from the seminary where Gary had graduated, flowed into the parking lot, smiles on their faces, pillows under their arms.

"It's sunny," one girl said. "We left gray snow on the ground."

"Look at that field," her classmate said. "Is that cotton?"

Pastor Jean drove up as I led them into the church building. "You got here early!" she said. "And not a minute too soon. Has Lois told you how hard we're going to work you?"

"Kids Camp, tutoring for testing, a worship service for high school students," Gary said, giving Jean a bear hug. "Does that cover it, Pastor?"

"That's a start," she said. "Let me show you around."

The worship area had been rearranged for the week, with tables and chairs set up on the sides. The students dumped sleeping bags and duffle bags onto the shiny floor, giving the space the look of a cluttered dorm room.

"Are we sure this is where we want to put them?" I whispered to Jean.

Jean smiled faintly, observing my discomfort. "This will be fine for a few days."

"No one's ever camped in our sanctuary before," I said. "Maybe we should have used that smaller area in the back."

"I don't think that would hold this group," she said. "Besides, that's where we've set up the one-on-one sessions. I've got seven middle-school students and five high-schoolers who need help with test prep."

"If they don't pass, we're less likely to keep the school open," I said to Marti, who walked up as Jean spoke.

"More importantly," Jean said, "if they don't pass, they're less likely to get a high-school diploma. They can't move on without doing well on this test."

That evening youth from throughout the parish gathered at the Baptist church downtown for a concert and taco supper. Gary told a story about a friend who had nearly drowned trying to help another guy who was drowning.

"You can't help each other out without getting an education," he said. "You save each other by finishing high school."

On Monday, Tammy grabbed her camera bag and followed a group who led reading classes at the public library and played volleyball in a neighborhood church gym.

"They're so genuine," she said, showing me her photographs. "I can't imagine giving up my vacation to help kids I don't know."

Armed with one of the *Item's* small digital cameras, Molly tagged along with a tutoring group and snapped shots that evening as they served free hot meals at the Methodist church. Marti directed this tribe, and I went along, watching my friend's easy smile and warm manner.

"When did you get so nice?" I asked, draping my arm over her shoulder.

"When you left town," she said. "When did you get so nice?"

We laughed at our silliness, old friends back together without missing a beat.

"I love the way you and Gary work as a team," I said.

"It takes a lot of juggling with my job at the *Post*," she said. "But I have to make ministry a priority. I use my vacation time on these trips, but it's well worth it. People at the *Post* don't understand, but it's more rewarding than a trip to a resort. I have fun doing this."

While we chatted, I watched Molly take pictures and smile shyly at some of the students, including a cute boy, two heads taller than she was, who bent down to hear what she was saying.

"Looks like Molly's making a new boyfriend," Marti gestured to the duo.

"I hope not. She's got a steady. Remember Anthony? The kid who got hurt playing basketball?"

"That guy?" Marti asked. I saw Anthony sitting in his wheelchair staring at Molly.

"Hey, Anthony, over here," I yelled with a smile. "Come meet my friend Marti."

He looked up, but instead of coming our way, he pushed away, brushing against the church door and heading down the ramp.

"He looks upset," Marti said.

I ran after him. "Anthony! Wait! What's going on?"

Almost to the curb, he stopped so suddenly that I nearly ran into the wheelchair. When I stepped in front of him, his face was defiant, but I could see tears in his eyes. "I can't hang around here anymore," he said. "I'm heading on home."

"Are you sick?" I asked. "Do you need me to call Dr. Kevin? Or drive you home?"

"Yes, I'm sick," he said, spinning his chair around, his muscular arms gleaming under the street light. "I'm sick of being dependent on everyone else. Sick of this thing."

He banged his hand against the chair arm. "Sick of holding Molly back."

"Whoa," I said as he started down the sidewalk again. "Is that what this is about?"

"I'm a loser," he said. "She's smart and talented and cute, and she spends all her time babysitting me, on top of working three jobs. It's not fair to her."

"Don't you think she should be the one to decide that?"

"She's too nice to break it off," he said. "Did you see her in there? She could have any boy in that room."

I smiled. Molly had always been shy and a little on the heavy side. She didn't exude confidence the way Katy did, but she had a sweet smile that let you know she was a listener.

"I'm glad you realize how special she is," I said after a moment. "That should make you even more thankful she chose you."

"That was before I got hurt." He rolled the chair a few inches down the sidewalk.

"Molly may be too good for you." I sat on the curb, and, as I hoped, my words stopped him, but he did not turn around. "She deserves someone who gives her credit for not turning her back on her friends, no matter what happens."

Anthony turned the chair around but did not come closer.

"Would you care about Molly if she were in that wheelchair?" I asked.

"Don't be stupid, Miss Lois," he said. "Of course I would. Nothing would make me quit caring for Molly."

I sat quietly as Pastor Jean had done so many times with me.

"It's hard," he said finally, wheeling up next to me. "At first, everyone came around, tried to cheer me up, even brought me presents. It was kind of like a party in a weird way. Then it turned into my everyday life."

My heart ached for the young man, and I tried to think what Chris might say. I knew my words mattered, and I looked down the street, collecting my thoughts.

I looked up at Anthony.

"That night at the hospital, when you were first injured, we thought you might die," I said. I could tell the words were not what he expected. They were not the words I had planned to say.

"You fought harder that night, and the next day, and the next, harder than anyone I had ever seen. You inspired your friends, cheered them up. You have helped Chris through your entire ordeal."

I nodded toward the church gymnasium. "That building is filled with great young people, but not one of them is any better than you. You light up a room, whether you're charging down a basketball court or holding your little brother in your lap."

"I might never charge down a basketball court again." His voice was solemn.

"No, you might not. But whatever you do, you'll do it with purpose and enthusiasm." I reached up to lay my hand on his arm.

"Molly may have told you that I'm an impatient sort of person. I sometimes wrestle with why God lets things happen. But you've already learned a lesson it took me much longer to get through my thick skull," I said.

He looked quizzical.

"You know you were created for something special."

He nodded his head slightly. "There's no going back, is there, Miss Lois?"

I shook my head.

"I can choose to be happy, right? Or be miserable that things didn't turn out the way I wanted."

"It's not easy," I said. "But it's the truth."

The glow of the streetlight, one of the vintage reproductions installed after the storm, illuminated Anthony's face. He looked like a modern angel, peace on his face.

"Shall we go back in?" I asked, my legs tingling as I rose from the curb.

"Want to race?" he asked.

———

Five days later the Ohio students gathered at Grace Chapel for their farewell service.

"We came down to Louisiana to give something away," one cute young girl with long curly hair said. "But we were blessed instead."

"We thought we were the ones with something to offer," a boy in an Ohio State T-shirt and jeans said. "But we were the ones in need."

One by one the students walked to the front of the worship area, now a conglomeration of sleeping bags and backpacks, Bibles, chairs, and a table here or there. They sang, they cried, they prayed.

As they finished, many of the Green students lined up along the wall, each holding a piece of colored poster board. "You gave me . . ." was printed in bold black marker on each poster. Randi, the girl I had seen in the school office, played the piano, and Molly began to sing a ballad about hope and love, about faith.

"I've never heard that before," I whispered to Pastor Jean, who stood near the back with me and Marti.

"Molly wrote it last night," Jean said.

While I soaked in the lyrics, the melody, the haunting holiness of the moment, the Green students began to move to the front of the worship area. Each briefly held up a sign, the words "You gave me . . ." front and center.

Slowly they turned the cardboard over to reveal the gifts they had received:

"Hope that I can graduate."

"Help with my math homework."

"Friendship with people from another state."

"Love when I felt lonely."

The signs were a rainbow of encouragement, one after another, some held by small children, their handwriting scrawled and hard to read, others by teens, trying to look cool but becoming emotional at the same time.

The last to join the group was Anthony, who smiled at Molly as he pushed himself to the front. He lifted his poster from his lap.

"You gave me . . ."

He turned it over.

"Courage to help others."

Molly finished her song and walked over to Anthony, handing him the microphone.

"We offer our thanks," he said. The crowd applauded, and some of the kids yelled out and whistled. "You changed our lives by giving of yourself."

18

*Wilderness Buddies will meet next Tuesday to hear
retired biologist Mickey McMillan demonstrate how to
prepare Paw-Paw Pudding and Wild Hog Head Boudin.
Mickey says his goal is to teach children how to eat from
the forest. His cookbook should be available soon. When
asked if he would show kids how to cook a raccoon, he
said, "We don't eat 'em. And, if we don't eat 'em,
we don't fix 'em."*

—*The Green News-Item*

Kevin decided we needed to learn how to quilt.

Tammy thought it was the funniest idea she'd ever heard. "You? Quilt? That reminds me of the time I was going to learn to rollerblade."

"Kevin thinks we need a hobby, something relaxing, where we can visit and accomplish something."

"Accomplish something?" Tammy snorted. "That's not a hobby, that's a to-do list."

Iris Jo had been quiet during the newsroom conversation, but she gave one of her small smiles. "I've always loved needlework. My grandmother made beautiful quilts."

"Aren't you part of the sewing group at Grace Chapel?" I asked. "Didn't you help with the dogwood wall-hanging for my wedding?"

"I stuffed the batting in that. I don't know any of the intricate stitching."

"Would you join us if we started a group?"

"I'd love to."

"You want to give it a try, Tammy?"

"It depends on when you have your meetings or whatever you call them. I like to stay home with Walt when I'm not working."

"You really have settled down," I said.

"Look who's talking," Tammy said. "You and Iris are as settled as they come."

"Isn't it nice?" Iris said.

"All three of us married in a year," I said.

"It changed our lives, didn't it?" Tammy said. "Maybe I will take up quilting."

———⊶⊷———

Kevin organized our group as though we were starting a new business, inviting me for a "planning meeting" before we got started. She dropped Asa off at her parents' house and presented me an array of catalogs and quilting books the minute I got to her house.

She tapped her hand on a legal tablet. "Here's a list of decisions we need to make."

"Do you mean like who's going to bring refreshments?"

"Would I ever plan a meeting with you that didn't include refreshments?" She smiled, her beautiful dark eyes shining. "We can meet at my house and decide what day we want to meet, the projects to sew, supplies we'll need, and the like. I can order what we come up with, or maybe Tammy will pick them up for us in Shreveport."

"I have an idea," I said.

She gave me a tiny frown. "This doesn't have to do with the school, does it?"

"The school? Of course not."

"You've been wrapped up with that for months now. I'm hoping this might take your mind off it for a while."

"That hurts my feelings," I said. "That's like me trying to tell you not to spend so much time at the hospital after the tornado."

"Which you did tell me," she said.

"Maybe so, but my idea doesn't have anything to do with schools. It has to do with who we might invite to be part of the quilting group." I tapped her notebook. "Start a list."

"How about Molly's mother, Esther? I've wanted to get to know her better," Kevin said.

"What a wonderful idea," I said. "Maybe Anthony's mother would come with her, and I'd like to ask Becca."

"The florist?"

I nodded. "She lives over in Ashland and seems to spend all her time working."

"Does she have a family?"

"I don't know much about her, but she acts like she wants to get involved in the community."

"She's done a beautiful job with her store," Kevin said. "My mother buys most of her gifts there, and the displays are stunning."

"Maybe she'll help us design our quilts." I pointed to a colorful photograph in a coffee table book. "What pattern is this?"

"That's a double wedding ring," Kevin said. "My great-aunt makes those when the kids in the family get married."

"Is she working on one for you and Terrence?" I asked.

"We're not serious," she said. "I don't have time to get serious."

"And that's why you're taking up quilting? Give that guy a chance."

"Is it just me or are you meddling again?" she asked, stacking the catalogs in neat piles.

"I know little A.C. brings you a lot of joy," I said, "but I hate to see you rule out getting married."

"I haven't ruled it out," she said, "but it's different when you have a child to consider. When I adopted Asa, I promised him he would always come first. How could I be the kind of wife I need to be and still give my son the attention he deserves?"

"People do it all the time," I said. "Look at your parents. I've never seen a more devoted couple than Marcus and Pearl, but they give you and their grandson love and attention."

"We'll see," she said. "Let's get back to our quilting."

Sometimes, despite my best efforts, I got so busy that I forgot to try new things. The quilting group turned out to be a fun experience, with an assortment of old and new friends.

At first Pastor Jean said no. "I'm too busy as it is," she said. "I need sleep more than I need to take up arts and crafts."

"Look at it this way," I said in her office at the church. "It'll be a gathering you don't have to organize, and we won't ask you to lead the prayer."

"Maybe I do need to try something different," she said. "I tend to get stuck in a rut. Plus, it'll help me quit missing Don so much. He was up here so much after the tornado that it's lonely without him."

I couldn't imagine spending days away from Chris. "The quilting group will be a good diversion" was all I could add.

I tried to talk Linda and Rose into coming, but they both said they were too busy with their day jobs and the shop. "The Holey Moley Antique Mall is my hobby," Rose said. "Ask me again when I retire."

Esther said a tentative yes. "Are you sure it'd be OK?" she asked, reminding me of her daughter's shyness.

"We'd be thrilled for you to join us," I said.

Anthony's mother jumped in immediately. "My grandma taught me to quilt when I was a girl, and I won a blue ribbon in the junior division at a county fair in Alabama." She grimaced. "Then I got off the straight and narrow and gave it up. Granny died the same month Anthony was born."

The hardest invitation went to Priscilla Robinson. Even the idea made my blood pressure rise.

"We're trying to bring women together. She's new to our community and needs friends," Kevin said. "Don't you remember what that felt like?"

"I wasn't trying to wreck the town when I got here, and I don't intend to be friends with her."

"You're open-minded, remember? The big-city chick who has the broad view of people."

"I don't like to be in the same room with that woman. I certainly don't want to let her have a pair of scissors when I'm around."

Kevin looked over her reading glasses at me and didn't say anything else.

"It won't work," I said.

A question mark wrinkled her brow. "What won't work?"

"That wise-woman look you're throwing at me. I know what you're doing. You're thinking if you give me that look and don't say anything, I'll agree."

The quiet look continued.

"We have a good group lined up already," I said. "We don't want it to get too big."

Kevin sighed. "Do you remember when you landed in Green and my parents invited you over to eat dinner? You said it was the best meal you'd ever had."

The memory of that invitation and that food still warmed my heart.

"My parents wanted you to know you were welcome here, whoever you were, wherever you came from. They twisted my arm to get there after work because they told me you needed a friend or two in Green."

"OK, OK, I surrender. But she won't come, and do I have to be the one to ask her?"

Kevin gave me one of the looks she gave Asa when he got into something he shouldn't.

"Don't you think you should?" she asked.

"You sound like my mother, your mother, Iris Jo, Pastor Jean, and my husband all rolled into one. I'll ask her, but I'm not sitting by her if she says yes."

❧

Priscilla didn't return three phone calls, and I tried to convince myself I had tried and could let it go. The thought of Kevin's disappointment in me, and her reminder of how people had welcomed me, wouldn't let me.

"Will you tell her I want to invite her to a party?" I asked the secretary on the fourth call.

"Miss Lois, I have given her your messages, word for word, but I'll be glad to tell her again." Her voice dropped. "I don't think she cares for the newspaper all that much."

The truth was the newspaper didn't care for her all that much either, but I held my tongue. "This isn't about the newspaper," I said. "We want to invite her to a community get-together at Dr. Kevin's."

The receptionist called back the next day, a spark of surprise in her voice. "Principal Robinson said she'll try to get by the doctor's house for a few minutes, but she can't stay long."

"She did?" I gasped.

The woman's voice lowered until I could barely hear it. "I heard her tell that consultant that she needs to see and be seen, whatever that means."

"I believe in some circles that's known as lobbying," I said. "Tell her we look forward to seeing her." I hoped she wouldn't show up.

I slipped into the back door of Kevin's clinic after a business meeting one afternoon and waved to one of the lab technicians to let them know I was there. I could hear the murmur of Kevin's voice in a room with a patient.

Scooting into her office, I sat down in the chair across from her desk, a gift when she had been chief resident in medical school. My eyes went immediately to a large bouquet of pink roses on top of a filing cabinet, a card pinned to the ribbon around the vase.

I made myself look away, at the clock, at crayon artwork taped to the wall, and the newest framed portrait of Asa, one of the cutest little boys ever, his burn scars hardly visible. I tried to ignore the flowers and stood up to examine a bulletin board filled with photographs of Kevin's young patients, thank-you notes and birth announcements mixed in.

The pungent smell of the flowers tickled my nose, and I eased my way behind the desk, casually picking up a book propped between bookends made of blue stone. With a medical book in hand, which even to me seemed like a ridiculous ploy, I craned my neck and read the note.

"I'll wait as long as it takes. Love, Terrence"

"Does snooping come naturally to you?" Kevin said, striding into the room, and I dropped the heavy medical book on my foot.

I yelped. "I think I broke my toe."

"Nice try, but you're not going to get any sympathy from me."

"I see why you were so familiar with the florist when I brought her name up for the quilting group," I said.

An odd sound like a mixture of a laugh and a sigh came from her. "Terrence is a thoughtful guy. He sends flowers pretty often."

"Here we go again," I said. "Give that man a chance. I can't recall the last time I got flowers from Chris."

"Lois, I've got eight patients in the waiting room, two to visit in the hospital, and a toddler son at home. Are you here for something special, or do you want to hound me about my love life?"

"I'd rather talk about your love life," I said, "but I stopped by to congratulate you on your great idea for the quilting circle. It struck a chord with everyone. I think they were hungry to get together."

"Why'd you think I had the idea in the first place?" she said. "I need my girlfriends."

Rose had an assortment of quilts on display in her store, and I contemplated the kind I wanted to make.

"This one has old feed sacks for its backing," she said, holding up a patchwork design in light blues and yellows, cotton batting sticking out in various spots.

"That pink one reminds me of spring," I said. "Look at how tiny the stitches are on those flowers."

"That's appliquéd," Rose said. "You put the design on the outside, instead of piecing it together. Here's another example with sunflowers."

As I picked up the worn green and yellow quilt, I could picture it draped over a chair in our new sunroom, the muted colors of the cotton complementing the crisp, fresh paint.

"I'm buying this one," I said. "I can decorate a whole room around it."

"That's the thing about quilts," Rose said, folding it with the care of a mother handling an infant. "They have personalities all their own and were made to be used. Every time I pick up one for the shop, I think about the women who made it, what they were like. Almost all of these quilts were made to keep somebody warm on a cold night or to celebrate an occasion."

During our first group meeting, the conversation turned to favorite quilts, and I was astonished at how quickly each woman mentioned one. "My grandma had one called 'the big cover,'" Esther said. "Molly slept under it when she was a baby, played with it, and used it for a tent. By the time my other babies came along, it was in shreds."

"My Granny made a purple quilt for me," Anthony's mother said. "It had little dolls in sunbonnets, like my grandmother wore when she worked in the garden or hung clothes out on the line."

When I glanced over at Iris Jo, I saw she was crying. "Some women at church made a baby blanket for me when Matt was born," she said. "After he died, I gave it away with his other things. I wish I had held on to it now."

"Asa has one, too, all soft like he is." Kevin said. "What was Matt's like?"

"It had sailboats on it," Iris said, wiping her eyes, "with bright red sails. I'm sorry for crying, but I had forgotten how much it meant to me."

Our lunchtime conversations at the *Item* revolved around quilting, too, with hours spent discussing favorite patterns and deep questions such as whether cotton or polyester batting was better and whether it was ever OK to machine stitch a quilt.

"You can't make everything about rules," Tammy said. "I can sew twice as many quilts if I use a machine."

"But this is supposed to be about love and care," I said. "If you want a bunch of bedspreads, run down the street and buy some."

"Why don't we ask our readers?" Iris interrupted our argument with her question. "Let's see what people in town say about their quilts. We can even get their quilting questions answered by someone."

"Pictures," Tammy interjected. "We can run pictures of favorite quilts with stories."

While the town had been interested in the school story, they were crazy about the quilt project. Everyone had a quilt, a quilt story, or a quilt photograph.

My favorite was a friendship quilt. A woman a little older than Iris brought her elderly mother to the newspaper, apologizing when I appeared in the lobby.

"I told Mama you were too busy to see her," she said, "but we had errands to run, and she insisted we stop by."

The woman, with a quilt draped over her walker, interrupted. "I told her you wouldn't have asked for quilts if you didn't want people to bring them. I'm Ida Montgomery," she said, "from around Cold Water. You're a lot prettier than your photograph, Miss Lois."

I fingered the quilt. "This is a treasure. Maybe we could get a picture of you holding it."

"Each square represents one of my friends from my young-married days," she said, beaming. "See how they embroidered their signatures, here, with the date. That's been more than fifty years ago." Her voice trailed off as her hands traced the different-colored threads.

"Lucille, here, died almost ten years ago. She loved flowers. Ruth left us about eight years ago. Heart attack. She baked pies for everyone."

A memory crossed her face. "This block is her cherry pie. Deborah made this square with the tree on it. She's in a nursing home now, doesn't remember who I am, but her daughter told me she still remembers our quilting circle."

Tammy photographed each square, and I wrote the story of the women who had created the work of art.

When we gathered at Kevin's house for our first meeting, the group came together like a circle of old friends reunited after a painful absence. Insistent on providing a meal for the debut of the club, Kevin beamed as she served a spiral-cut ham and her version of her mother's potato salad.

"I doctor it to give it my own flavor," she said to Iris Jo.

"Doctor it?" I groaned, as the doorbell rang.

"Instead of making fun of me," Kevin said, "why don't you get the door?"

Priscilla Robinson stood under the porch light, an uneasy expression on her face and a small gift bag in her hand.

"For the hostess," she said, looking over my shoulder as though assessing an audience.

"How nice," I said, taking the present and wondering why I hadn't thought to bring something.

The women, who were nestled in groups of two or three chatting about crafts, families, and, of course, the school, grew silent as the principal took off her coat.

"This was a mistake," she mumbled as she looked for a place to put her purse, and for a split second I thought she'd walk out the door.

"Priscilla, welcome," Kevin said, wiping her hands on an embroidered dishtowel as she emerged from the other room.

The administrator displayed a standard meet-and-greet smile. "Hello, Doctor," she said.

My best friend laughed. "Call me Kevin. Pastor Jean, would you make sure everyone knows everyone?"

When I glanced at Kevin, I could tell she didn't quite trust me to guide the administrator into the group. Helping put the food on the table, I watched Priscilla, her back stiff, ease through the room as though she could step on a steel trap at any moment.

But even with her sharp edge, she had done her homework. She talked with Anita about Anthony's therapy and complimented Iris Jo on her work with the Booster Club. She asked Jean a question about settling into the new church and complimented Kevin on the spring decorations she had placed around her home.

Suspicious, I waited for her to slip, to pry about the school situation or launch into a tirade about how important the closing of the Green School was, but the subject was never raised, her gaze only wary when she caught me staring at her.

"Lois?" Kevin's voice broke through my wandering mind, and I noticed she was holding up my laptop computer. "Do you want to show the friendship quilt squares from the paper?"

Going through the photographs that would run next week, I talked about each square, noticing two or three of the new quilters wiping their eyes as I told the stories. A deep affection welled in my heart, for the women who had made the old quilt and for these new friends in Kevin's living room.

"Let's do one of those," Anita said when I finished. "I want to do a square with a basketball and Anthony's jersey."

"We can all choose our color schemes and make squares for each other," Kevin said, practically dancing around the room.

"We'll draw names to see what order we go in. I'm going to do Xs and Os, hugs and kisses for Asa Corinthian."

"I'm going to do a sailboat," Iris said, "in memory of Matt."

"I'll do a camera," Tammy said.

"What will you do, Miss Robinson?" Anthony's mother asked.

The question caught Priscilla off guard. "Oh, I won't be a part of the group. I don't plan to be in Green very long."

The remark brought a quiet murmur, as though reminding the women why she was in town in the first place.

"Pastor?" Kevin asked, breaking up the awkward moment.

"I'd like to do a church, like the old Grace Chapel," Jean said.

"Lois?" Tammy said. "We haven't heard your idea yet."

I looked around the living room, a dozen ideas whirling through my mind. A schoolhouse. Chickens. A cute white dog. A front page of *The Green News-Item*. A pink dogwood bloom. The state of Louisiana with a heart up north where Green was.

"Earth to Lois," Tammy said. "What are you going to do for your theme?"

"A cup."

"A cup?" Tammy's Lois-doesn't-have-a-clue voice was evident.

"For all that coffee you drink?" Iris asked, her tone kind as always.

I looked at the women—the mother, whose son my husband coached and loved; the newspaper staff members, who somehow got our little paper out; my pastor, who kept teaching me about loving others and loving myself; the doctor, who knew my heart as though we had been friends for decades. Even this outsider who challenged me in ways I didn't care for.

"A cup," I said again. "Because my cup runneth over."

⸺⊛⸺

Iris popped into my office the next morning as soon as I arrived and closed the door, which always meant something was up.

"I'm excited about the friendship quilt," she said. "I can't wait to do my squares."

"It's a piece of history, isn't it?" I wondered why she was really here.

"The only thing is, I need to make another quilt, too," she said, moving from one foot to the other in a motion that seemed more like Tammy than Iris.

"Oh, did you find another pattern you like?"

"I need a new baby quilt," she said. "I'm sort of old for this, but Stan and I are going to have a baby."

19

How romantic is this? Wedding bells are going to be ring-
ing for Scarlett Kelley and her boyfriend Rhett Dalzell.
With those names, they had to fall in love! These two met
while working together at a camp outside Breaux Bridge.
They hope to find teaching jobs at Green High in the fall.

—The Green News-Item

Katy called a producer from a national network about the march to Baton Rouge.

"He's going to contact their affiliate in New Orleans," she said. "We can probably at least get regional coverage."

Finished with her freshman year in college, she was home for a month before heading to New York for another magazine internship. Molly was going to summer school, but her classes were online, and she planned to add to her babysitting hours for Asa and work more at the *News-Item*.

"Can you get cold feet about staging a protest walk?" Molly asked from the composing room area. "I'm not cut out for television."

"What's the purpose of doing it if you don't tell the world?" Katy asked.

"To make a point?" Molly said.

"That, too," Katy said and sashayed across the room to grab Molly. "You're my hero." She pulled back. "But did you have to invite Mr. Ellis to go with us?"

Molly laughed. "He sort of invited himself."

"Eugene got fed up with Priscilla telling him what to do," Chris said during one of our evening walks. "He has lots of connections in Baton Rouge, so it's probably a good thing he's going."

Staging the walk was a lot more intricate than it had seemed at first. Tammy insisted on staying with the trio the entire way, outlining her plans in my office. "It's historic, and I couldn't live with myself if something happened to them. I know how to take care of myself."

"That you do," I said, recalling her baseball-bat attack. "That you do."

Iris Jo identified restaurants, booked hotels along the way, and contacted school Booster Clubs to turn out and show their support.

Walt, Chris, and I divided up car duty to check on the walkers along the way.

Linda talked Doug into asking his law-enforcement contacts to keep an eye on the group. "He isn't happy about them being on the road," she said, "but he'll make sure his colleagues know they're passing through."

Katy, flush with her success with the television station and her good grades in her college debut, looked up every newspaper, radio station, and television studio between Green and Baton Rouge and let them know about the walk. "We're fighting for our school," she said, time and again. "We'd love to give you exclusive coverage when we pass through your community."

"Katy, it's not exclusive coverage if you give it to everyone," I told her firmly.

She ran her fingers through her short hair, now blond, and grinned. "Everyone will get a special interview."

The Green High Booster Club orchestrated the sendoff from the front of the school on a Saturday morning, with members of a community band playing songs like "Battle Hymn of the Republic."

Katy's stepfather's office had refused our request for a gathering on the lawn of the school, but had told her privately he couldn't stop us from meeting on the sidewalk.

Linda, Eugene's wife, and I followed the quartet for the first few miles.

"We'll come see you this evening," I promised and felt oddly bereft as I saw Molly waving in the rearview mirror.

Tammy called on the hour every hour, sometimes with better cell-phone reception than others. "It's unbearably hot," she said on the second day. "Maybe we should have ridden bicycles or something."

"Did you know Molly had arranged for her classmates at the junior college to show up in Alexandria?" Katy asked, a hint of pride in her voice. "They held signs and cheered when we went through town."

"Molly doesn't talk much about her classes down there," I said and realized I knew more about Katy's studies in Georgia than I did about Molly's. "She certainly juggles a lot."

By Day Three, the four were celebrities, with a video clip posted on the Internet by Katy's friends at college and picked up by two national cable shows. A syndicated radio program asked them to call along the way. A blogger with a national following depicted Eugene Ellis as an aging giant who had worked hard for students his entire life and who refused to be pushed around as he prepared for retirement.

"Everyone loves Mr. Ellis," Katy gushed when Iris, Jean, and I drove down for a highway visit that evening. "He's like a teddy bear with a brain."

Eugene laughed and excused himself. "This is the most fun I've had in a long time, but I'd better give my wife a call and hit the hay."

Katy continued her description of the day's activities, with Tammy jumping in occasionally and Molly smiling and rubbing her feet.

"Molly says she doesn't like TV cameras, but she charms everyone," Tammy said.

"Even being on television beats walking," Molly said.

By the fifth day, the mission had gained momentum, and the three attended an impromptu party for education north of Lafayette. "We lost our school last year," the mayor of a small town said, "and you make me realize we should have tried harder to save it."

"We don't have any guarantee of success," Eugene said, "but these young women have reminded me that at least we can take a stand."

When they cut through on a smaller highway, the trio was mobbed by fans, including a teachers' sorority and a parents' club. The crowd grew so large that Doug called Linda to complain.

"His buddies say they didn't count on this," the reporter told me, "and this is a public-safety hazard."

I sighed. "He's probably right."

Katy and Tammy posted items on the *News-Item* website each evening, and comments grew and grew.

Some were glowing. "It's nice to see young people leading the way," one man wrote.

"Eugene Ellis continues to show why he's the best educator in Louisiana," another reader said.

Others took shots at James and the school board. "If the school superintendent did his job, those little girls wouldn't have to risk their lives to make a statement." "That twit of a new principal should be fired," another said.

I monitored the remarks constantly and tried to delete the rude ones, with Linda occasionally fussing at me. "If we're going to let the public speak its mind, we can't delete harsh comments," she said.

"*Anonymous* harsh comments," I said. "Anyone can sling mud when they don't have to sign their name."

"We're hypocrites if we censor people," she said.

"They're hypocrites if they won't sign their names."

Originally we estimated the walk would take two weeks, but the pace slowed as the group continued. "Do you want to ride part of the way?" I asked Molly after a week-and-a-half. "Maybe walk the last leg into the capital?"

"We talked about that," she said, "and decided it's all or nothing."

"Those girls are fighters," Eugene said. "I'd probably have taken the ride, but they'd shame me."

As they drew closer, we had to decide two things: how to get them across the Mississippi River without endangering lives and how they could maximize their impact on state government.

Doug solved the bridge dilemma by arranging a security escort.

"It was creepy," Molly said. "I couldn't look down from the bridge."

"It reminded me of being on a Ferris wheel," Katy said.

"I'd rather not think about it," Eugene said.

Chris took one of his few personal school holidays for the final segment, and he, Walt, Linda, and I met up with the walkers in the least expensive hotel Iris could find in the vicinity of the capitol. This was my first trip to Baton Rouge.

We gathered in the lobby, preparing for the next day. A few guests, including lobbyists and businesspeople, stopped to say hello.

"I've been waiting all week for you to get here," a representative from a teacher's union said. "It's about time someone stood up for our schools."

"Isn't that what you're supposed to do?" Tammy muttered, and I poked her in the side.

"We all need to do our part," Katy said, sounding like she was twenty years older than she was.

"I couldn't have said it better," Mayor Eva said, strolling into the hotel with Dub and Joe behind her.

"Nor I," Pastor Jean said, pushing Anthony through the automatic doors, behind her husband and Molly's mother.

"What are you doing here?" Molly jumped up, as though she were sitting on hot coals. "Mama, who's got the little kids?"

"Dr. Kevin and her parents are keeping an eye on them," Molly's mother said. "She said you always help her out, and she wanted to do something nice for you."

"Don't you have school tomorrow?" Molly said to Anthony, trying to sound mad as she rushed over to him.

"I told the principal I was taking a field trip," he said. "I got most of my work done ahead of time."

Chris and I arrived at the capitol before the others the next day, and I gulped as I looked up at the tall limestone tower against the bright blue sky.

"It looks like the Empire State Building," I said, admiring the wide stairs leading to the entrance; the lush, broad lawn; and the well-tended flower beds edging up to the sidewalks.

"Huey Long, governor at the time, had the idea to build it," Chris said, squeezing my hand. "A few years later he was

223

assassinated in its corridors and is buried here. The governor's mansion is over there." He pointed. "Don't get any ideas about us living there one day."

"I don't want to be a politician," I said. "Just a newspaper owner and coach's wife."

"I know my wife. First she gets me to the steps of the capitol, the next thing I know I'm moving to Baton Rouge."

As we stood on the lawn, waiting for Molly, Katy, and Eugene, people dressed in green began to trickle out of the entrance and to walk around the corners of the building.

"I've never had so much trouble finding a parking place," my banker, Duke, said.

"You should have ridden the bus with us," Bud said, Anna Grace holding onto his arm.

"Except its air conditioner didn't work," my mother-in-law said, coming across the lawn as though she went to the capitol every day.

"Your walkers have quite a fan club," Eva said, wearing a tailored green dress.

"Oh, thank you," I prayed and regretted again the years I had let slip by without gratitude for all the good in my life.

Molly, Katy, and Eugene had dressed up for the last few blocks of their journey, clothed in green dress-up clothes and athletic shoes. "I didn't want to show up looking like a hobo," Mr. Ellis said, and the girls agreed that they wanted to show Green in the best possible light.

The crowd parted and clapped as the trio climbed the first thirteen steps, designed to commemorate the first thirteen states. They paused on a small platform before tackling the remaining thirty-five, symbolizing the rest of the states at the time of construction.

I noticed Eva talking on the phone before she turned to join in the cheering. Molly nudged Mr. Ellis forward, but he shook his head and held his hand out to her.

"May I introduce to you the young woman who has led us here today," he said. "Molly Moore. Student, advocate, friend of education."

"I thank you all for coming," the young woman said. "A community's school is part of its heart and soul. Perhaps we can't save Green's schools forever, but we want to keep them as long as we possibly can. We're here to ask the legislature to take another look at how it funds small schools and do what it can for us."

The crowd applauded.

"We know it's not easy, but we hope each person will do their part, step by step, as we have walked here, to our beautiful state capitol."

At that moment the governor stepped outside.

20

*Talk about making a beeline! That's what O.M. Hart did
when he was stung while clearing land on Route Two.
"The worst part was when the bees followed me into the
cab of my truck and kept on stinging me," he said. "I've
mowed past that hive a hundred times, but I won't ignore
it again, that's for sure."*

—The Green News-Item

Everyone except Chris seemed edgy during the last week of
the school year—and what could be the last week of the Green
school.

"If this door closes, another will open," he said, hanging
wooden blinds in the den.

"Do you believe that?" I asked, sitting on the edge of a chair
covered with plastic.

"Absolutely."

"But aren't you the least bit uncertain?"

"Only about getting these blinds up like I promised you."
He tilted his head. "Does this look straight?"

"It's perfect," I said, drinking in his ragged gray T-shirt and
the look of concentration on his face.

⟐⟐⟐

"Have we heard anything?" I asked when Linda stepped into the newsroom on Monday.

She shot me a look similar to one of Tammy's favorites. "Lois, did I promise to call you if I heard anything?"

"Yes."

"Have I called you?"

"No."

"That means we haven't heard anything," Tammy said, walking in on the end of the conversation.

"Aren't you two the least bit worried?" I asked.

"I quit worrying about things I can't control," Linda said. "It kept upsetting my stomach."

"Speaking of upset stomachs, has anyone seen Iris Jo this morning?" Tammy asked.

"She had her standing doctor's appointment," I said.

"I wish she'd find out whether it's a boy or a girl," Tammy said.

"She and Stan are so thrilled they don't care what sex it is," I said. "I want them to get their house finished before he or she is born. I want to be able to walk down the road and hold it."

The phone rang, and Tammy stepped over to my desk to answer it. "It's Priscilla Robinson for Lois Craig," she said, holding out the receiver like it was a dead animal.

I snatched the phone from Tammy's hand. "Have they decided?"

"I'm afraid there's been a delay," Priscilla said. "I've been summoned back to Baton Rouge to appear before the committee again."

"Why are they dragging their feet?"

"Frankly, Lois, you should be gratified that they're holding out hope. This state hasn't reversed a school-closing in the past three decades, but at least they're being meticulous about their stance."

"So you think they're going to stick with their original opinions?" I asked.

"I doubt even the legislative body knows that. Dr. Hillburn says no new legislators have announced where they stand."

When I hung up, I looked at Tammy and Linda.

"How can they stand anywhere but for our school, our children?" I asked.

"Don't forget some of these lawmakers didn't save their own schools," Linda said. "They'll need a lot of courage to support Green."

"So much for that," Tammy said. "If it won't get them re-elected, they probably won't do it."

"We only have a week left before the children get out for the summer," I said. "It'd be nice if they knew something before they left."

"Miss Priss probably wants it this way," Tammy said. "That way she doesn't have the tears flowing when everyone leaves the last time. All nice and neat."

"Maybe she's trying to do her job," I said. "She seems nice enough at the quilting circle, and I'm not sure she has that much sway in Baton Rouge."

"I don't know about her," Linda said, "but Marcus Hillburn seems to have a lot of clout. He wines and dines half of Baton Rouge."

"On the taxpayers' expense account," I grumbled.

"That's it!" Linda said. "I should have listened to Alex in the first place."

She hurried from the room, Tammy on her heels.

By the time I got into the newsroom, Linda was sitting on the floor, her education files spread out in a row of new stacks, copies of reports lined up by year.

"Did I miss something?" I asked.

"You told me to look at the money," the reporter said, "but I was looking at the wrong money. It's the travel expenses, among other things."

The next day's edition carried the latest installment in Linda's ongoing school series, this one outlining how Marcus had charged three different school districts for the same expenses and taken government staff members to expensive restaurants, listing the meals as office supplies and curriculum expenditures.

"I had most of this worked out," Linda said that evening, "but I couldn't figure out the last piece. All I need is a comment from him. Do you want to place that call?"

I smiled and read back over her story. "You've more than earned the right to do that."

Marcus threatened to sue the paper and called the mayor's office.

"This hurts me more than I thought it would," Eva said when I called to check on her. "How could I have chosen to marry someone like that?"

"You were young, and he misled you," I said.

"I used bad judgment," she said, haltingly. "Lois, what if I'm doing that again?"

"Again? You're a great mayor," I said.

"I mean with Dub. What if he hasn't changed the way he says he has?"

The irony of my trusting Dub more than she did was not lost on me.

Marcus had left four messages on my voice mail before I got to work the next morning. In one of the messages, his words a little slurred, he tried to place the blame on Priscilla.

"She's setting me up because I ended our personal relationship," he said. "We made a good team for a while, but she was too needy."

When I called him back, he ranted and raved. "You're not doing the people of Green any good. They deserve more than some rinky-dink school that runs on a shoestring."

"They deserve more than an expensive consultant who wastes their hard-earned money," I said.

Priscilla called to demand that Linda and I come to her office before the paper was printed. "I do not want the good name of this school besmirched by your innuendoes."

The school office was quiet when we arrived. The student worker who had taken my call that first day in January was stapling pages together. "Miss Robinson said she'd be back in a few minutes," the girl said. "You can have a seat in her office."

As I followed Linda out of the little lobby, the girl called my name, and I turned.

"Thank you for trying to save our school," she said.

When Priscilla swept into the office, she was talking on a high-end cell phone, a smudge on her pale yellow blouse. "You're breaking up," she said. "I can't make out what you're saying."

Apparently the caller dropped her because she hurled the phone across the room. I winced, and Linda froze. After months of control, Priscilla had snapped.

"I hope you're happy," Priscilla barked. "You've managed to undo months of hard work. The committee said they won't need my input for a decision after all."

"So they've made up their minds?" I asked.

She shook her head and almost seemed to deflate before my eyes. "They'll have an answer by the time they adjourn."

Linda looked at her watch. "We still have time to make today's edition. May I quote you on that?"

"Ask me anything," Priscilla said. "I just heard the sound of the door slamming on my career, anyway."

As the reporter rushed out to get the story written, I stood in the small entryway. "I suppose you know Marcus is blaming this on you," I said.

"I've heard," she said, sitting at the desk, her head in her hands. "But he's the one who stole your stupid old photographs. He's the one who wanted dirty tricks. I just wanted a promotion."

"He says you'll get a bonus from his firm if the school closes."

She moaned.

"I hope that's not true," I said and walked out.

———— ✎ ————

The *News-Item* GED graduation reception was Friday night at the country club, the evening before Green High commencement services.

We still had not gotten official word on whether we could keep our school or not, but the atmosphere in the room was cheerful.

Kevin, stunning in a black-and-white wrap dress, came in with Terrence, the evening's guest speaker. Asa Corinthian wore a miniature white suit and held onto Terrence's hand, breaking free to greet Anthony's little brother, Adam.

Tammy and Walt were visiting with Walt's parents, who had insisted on driving down for the event. "We are so proud of our daughter-in-law," said Walt Sr., the newspaper's former lawyer and long-ago love of my dear friend Aunt Helen. "We wouldn't have missed this for the world."

"Tammy is as smart as a whip," Walt's mother said, putting her arm around the younger woman's waist. "Did you know she's teaching me how to take digital photographs?"

Beaming, Tammy kissed the woman on the cheek. "You have a natural eye," she said.

Walt walked over to where Chris and I stood nearby. "Thanks for making this happen. I can scarcely imagine the doors you have opened through this class."

Mary Frances, pianist from Grace Chapel, played "Pomp and Circumstance" as those who had passed the test came to the front of the room to receive a certificate and a small gift, donated by Becca's shop. Only one of the *Item's* class members had failed, and she had promised Tammy she'd study harder next time.

Most of the participants brought their families for the program. Still in a wheelchair, Anthony looked strong and cheerful, clapping when his mother walked to the front.

"My mom graduated before me," he said afterwards with a giant smile. "That's the way it should be."

"Tomorrow's your big day, Son," Anita said. "Then we'll see who gets their college degree first."

Less than a year ago, Anita had been cowed by her abusive boyfriend, but she looked ten years younger tonight in a new peach-colored outfit. Anthony's little sister and brother also wore new clothes. "Iris and Stan bought these for us as a graduation gift," she said.

Iris leaned over and kissed the top of Alicia's head. "These two sweet children have opened doors for Stan and me," she said. "They made me remember how special it is to have children nearby."

The next morning I couldn't help myself. I let Holly Beth out and called Linda.

"Have we heard anything?"

"Lois, it's Saturday morning," she said. "Of course we haven't heard anything."

"They must be waiting until after graduation to drop the bomb."

"Wait and see," she said. "Wait and see."

The school auditorium smelled like lemon oil, and Becca was placing the last long white gladiolus in a copper container of greenery at the front when Chris and I showed up for graduation.

"Do you like it?" she said, pulling out a stalk, snipping it with her clippers and repositioning it. "I put in a special request with my wholesaler, and he came through. Green and white."

She reached into a wicker basket and pulled out a small flower box. "I have something for you, too, Lois."

Inside was a gardenia corsage with a green ribbon, the flower traditionally worn by Green graduates. "I thought you deserved this after all you did for the school."

"It might have all been for nothing," I said. "They still haven't made a decision."

She attached the corsage to the lapel of my light jacket. "Whatever happens, it wasn't for nothing," she said. "You did your best. What more could anyone ask?"

Chris headed toward the podium, and I looked around for my friends. The band struck up the school song, the crowd stood, and the graduates, wearing green caps and gowns, gardenias pinned to the girls' gowns, walked in.

Tammy laid her camera on the floor and let out one of her shrill whistles.

Katy, Molly, and Linda stood a few rows over from me and Iris, and Chris, wearing a coat and tie, was ready to pass out diplomas.

Only Priscilla Robinson didn't look relaxed.

The scent of the gardenia pinned on my dress wafted up.

"I think I have something in my eye," I whispered to Iris Jo with a sniff. She smiled and dug a Kleenex out of her purse.

As he had the year before, Katy's stepfather spoke at commencement. "This has been a year filled with struggles within our school district," James said, "but our graduates have never let themselves be derailed. They take the powerful gift of education with them."

The superintendent started to take his seat and then stood again, moving back to the microphone. "I feel as though I must apologize to each of you for any wrong I have done in not fighting harder for this school. No matter what happens in the future, I commit myself to making this a better place to live, to being a stronger leader."

I held my breath, wondering how the townspeople would react, but a hearty round of applause greeted his words.

They had accepted his apology.

Eugene Ellis walked front and center next. "It is my honor to present the Teacher of the Year honors for this school year," he said. "The award goes to someone who exemplifies what it means to be a teacher, a person who not only values the importance of learning but also offers each student kindness and respect." Eugene turned slightly. "Coach Chris Craig."

The crowd rose to its feet, clapping, and Chris looked overwhelmed. Katy acted as though she were high-fiving me across the room, and Molly gave a thumbs-up sign.

"Now I really have something in my eye," I said to Iris, smiling and dabbing at the tears. "Why didn't anyone tell me?"

"We wanted it to be a surprise," she whispered.

Chris wiped his hand down his face as he approached the microphone and cleared his throat.

"I'm stunned," he said. "It's pretty obvious my wife didn't know about this." The audience chuckled. "One of the great privileges of my life is to coach and teach. I work alongside an excellent group of teachers, each of whom deserves this honor. Whatever happens with our school, nothing will take away our commitment to help each child become what he or she was meant to be."

I sniffed again.

"He's a fine man," Iris said quietly. "I'm so happy you two found each other."

"Not half as happy as I am."

The band started playing "Pomp and Circumstance," like the evening before. The graduates stood, and Anthony steered his wheelchair to the back of the line. One by one the students took their diplomas, shaking hands and hugging the assorted faculty members and administrators.

As the class wound across the stage, Anthony seemed to park at the bottom of the ramp, and his mother stepped out of the crowd to stand by him. He was not moving toward the stage when his name was called, and I stiffened, nervous for him.

Slowly, Anthony got up from the wheelchair and grabbed the banister, taking one cautious step at a time. Even from where we sat, I could see sweat on his forehead.

The crowd jumped to its feet, and Tammy's whistles were joined by many others.

"Anthony Cox," Miss Robinson called out again, and Chris held the diploma and put his other hand on the young man's shoulder. He spoke into Anthony's ear, and both of them appeared to be crying.

Steadying himself, Anthony waved his diploma in the air and walked across the stage to the ramp where his mother waited, both of them beaming. The crowd continued to cheer, and Anthony sank back into his wheelchair, waving his diploma a time or two and then wheeling over to his classmates.

Eugene retrieved the microphone. "This year, as we give diplomas, we have an unexpected gift."

My heart leapt.

"Anonymous donors in the community have announced the establishment of the Helen McCuller Scholarship Fund, and the first recipient is Anthony Cox."

The crowd roared again. "Anthony, your full college expenses will be paid."

Helen McCuller, the woman who had taught me so much when I moved to Green. The woman who had given me my house, the house that had helped me get to know Chris down the road. She had died too soon.

I looked across the big room, my eyes magnetically drawn to Dub McCuller. A small smile crossed his face.

As everyone settled back into their seats after the scholarship announcement, I glanced at my staff members and saw Linda jerk her head, look down at her phone, write something, and tear out the sheet of paper.

She walked around the rear of the room and came up to the end of my row, squatting in the aisle and passing the paper to me, her face giving nothing away.

A knot formed in my stomach as I opened the note.

"We heard something," she had written. "It's going to make you very happy."

Our impromptu party had already begun by the time Chris and I arrived at our house. Mr. Hugh stood on the edge of the front porch, smiling and gesturing at Dub and Joe, who faced the house.

Katy and Molly stood by one of our seemingly limitless five-gallon buckets, a paintbrush in Katy's hand. Lee Roy Hicks was washing his hands at an outdoor faucet.

Estelle sat in the swing, Holly Beth next to her and a small package in her lap.

Maria and her boys wrestled with a long sheet of newsprint, the three bigger dogs running around it, trying to grab the ends.

Chris tapped the horn twice and waved. The men on the porch stepped back, revealing the house's original door, newly refinished and hung in its rightful place.

"Happy graduation day," my husband said, leaning over to kiss me.

"You redid the old door. It's beautiful."

"Lee Hicks did that," he said. "He took it on as a special thank-you project, saying you opened doors for him by accepting him in our home."

Sunlight bounced off the deep colors of the antique stained glass. I swallowed back tears.

"Do you like it?" Chris asked, gentle in tone. "I want this to be a special day for you."

"We're supposed to be celebrating your award and the wonderful news about the school," I said. "This is *your* day."

He shook his head. "You're the one who makes things happen."

As I climbed out of the old pickup, Joe stepped off the porch to help Maria with the paper, a long banner painted in green with smiling rabbits on each end. "Home of Lois Craig, honorary Green High Grad," it read.

Chris walked around the truck and took my hand. He looked in my eyes as though we were in the middle of our wedding ceremony.

"I love you so much," he said.

As we embraced, his mother walked across the yard, Holly Beth at her heels.

"I have a gift for you, Lois." Estelle handed me a small jewelry box.

Inside was a traditional Green High class ring with "1942" on it and "Estelle" engraved inside in tiny script.

"I want you to have this," my mother-in-law said. "You are such a blessing in our lives."

Chris took the ring and slipped it on my right hand. As tears ran down my face, he kissed me and held me close. "I can't wait to see what's next," he said.

I had a pretty good idea, but decided to wait to tell him.

Discussion Questions

1. *Rally 'Round Green* opens in the gym at Green School. What does the Rabbit Rally tell you about the community and about Lois? Two new characters, Marcus Hillburn and Priscilla Robinson, are introduced in the early chapters. What is your reaction to them? How do Lois and other residents of Green respond to them? Who do you like most in Green? Why do they appeal to you?

2. Lois and Chris Craig are remodeling an old house that needs lots of work. What doubts do the newlyweds experience as they work on the home, and what joys do they encounter? Was moving the house to the vacant lot and undertaking the project a good idea or not? Will Lois learn to love the home the way she loved Aunt Helen's cottage, where she used to live?

3. In each book in The Green Series, Lois faces unexpected challenges and blessings. What are rough situations she addresses in *Rally 'Round Green*? How does she grow from her fourth year in Green? In what ways does she need to continue to grow?

4. Mayor Eva Hillburn finds herself in the midst of three unusual relationships in her life. In what ways are her interactions with Dub McCuller, Major Wilson, and Marcus Hillburn similar? In what ways are they different? What tips would you give Eva on how to deal with these interesting men in her life?

5. Who do you consider the "bad guys" in this story? Why? What motivates them to do things that you might find distasteful? Do they have good qualities, also? If so, what are those qualities? Who are the most honorable people in the story?

6. What changes do Lois and her friends face in *Rally 'Round Green*? How do the Route Two building changes,

including the highway project, church move, and others, affect Lois? Do you encounter ongoing changes in your life? How do you deal with those? What suggestions could you offer on how to deal with tough changes?

7. Hard questions are raised about the future of Green School, and people talk about what the school means to them. Why do they care so much about their school? Do you have special memories of schools in your hometown? How did your education affect your life?

8. How do you feel about how *The Green News-Item* and the townspeople handle the issue of education? What challenges face education in your area? In what ways might you help people who need to learn to read or to get their GED? Is having a school in Green a clear-cut issue or does it have layers?

9. Katy and Molly are college students in this book. How are their lives similar? How do they differ? How do they learn from each other? Have you ever had a friend who helped you look at the world differently? What do you think will happen to these young women as they continue to mature?

10. Tammy, newspaper clerk and photographer, is adapting to her new marriage and keeping a secret. She also feels she is not worthy of her new husband, Walt, an attorney. What do you think about her struggles? Have you had times in your life when you felt as though you did not fit in? How did you handle those? How is Iris Jo adapting in *Rally 'Round Green*? In what ways are Tammy and Iris Jo connected, and how do they help Lois on her journey?

11. Anthony, Molly's boyfriend and one of Chris's students, faces unexpected adversity. How does he handle his problems? In what ways does his situation touch others in town? Is there someone in your church, neigh-

borhood, or community who needs encouragement or other help from you as they deal with an accident or illness?

12. Dr. Kevin brings a group of women together to work on a craft. Why does she want to do this? How might these women help each other? In what ways are members of the group similar and how do they differ? Do you have a group you get together with regularly? How do those people help you? What tips would you offer to someone who wants to start a small group?

13. Employees of the Green newspaper believe in making things happen. How does that affect Lois? What are examples of ways the staff helps the community in *Rally 'Round Green*? Can you give an example from your life when you felt moved to action? What was the outcome?

14. Marti was Lois's best friend in Ohio. How has their friendship changed since Lois moved to Green? How have your friendships changed through the years? How does Lois feel when Marti suggests a mission trip to Green, and why does Lois react the way she does? How did the trip work out? How might you pull a group together to help someone in need?

15. Relationships are at the heart of life in Green. Lois interacts with a variety of people, from a former hurtful employee to staff members who need her to her new in-laws. How would you describe Lois and the people she cares about? As life unfolds in Green, how do you see Lois growing and changing?

"Love You. Love You More."

An original quilt pattern for readers of the Green Series

By Mary Dark, co-author with Judy Christie of "Awesome Altars: How to Transform Worship Space"
(Abingdon Press, 2005)
www.altarworks.com

When Dr. Kevin Taylor of Green invites a group of women to join a quilting group, she wants a special quilt pattern to show her love for her adopted son, Asa Corinthian—a pattern that symbolizes hugs and kisses.

Mary Dark, who lives in Northwest Louisiana and leads classes nationwide in designing church altars, created this quilt pattern in memory of her mother-in-law and calls it, "Love You. Love You More."

The pattern can be enlarged to the size you desire, and Mary recommends using freezer paper because it is stiff and holds up well.

Have fun, and be sure to send a photo of your quilt to judy@judychristie.com! Mary and Judy would love to see it!

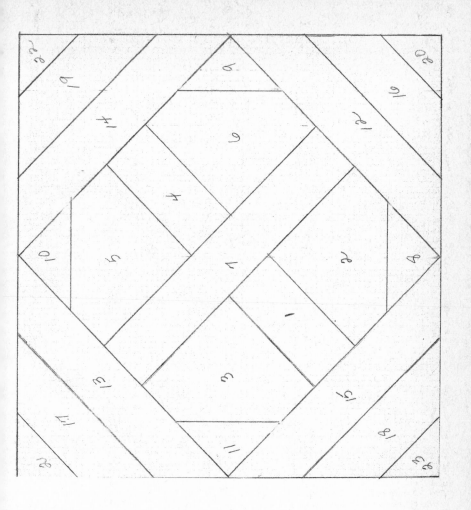

꒞꒰꒞꒰꒞꒰꒞꒰꒞꒰꒞꒰꒞꒰꒞꒰꒞꒰꒞꒰꒞꒰꒞꒰꒞꒰꒞꒰꒞꒰꒞

Some Green Recipes

Church Potluck Sweet Potato Pie

Grace Community Chapel celebrates its new building with a special service and a big potluck lunch afterwards. One of the favorites is sweet potato pie, a Louisiana specialty often served at Thanksgiving and other special occasions. This recipe is from Ethel Ransburg, a nurse and mother of five, and her daughter Eleanor, the kinds of cooks you want to be friends with!

Ingredients:

    3 sweet potatoes
    1½ sticks butter
    1¾ cups sugar
    ¾ teaspoon cinnamon
    ⅛ teaspoon nutmeg
    1½ teaspoon vanilla
    3 large eggs
    2 pie shells (8-inch)

Instructions:

Use small to medium-size potatoes. If you use really big potatoes or yams, you'll have to add more flavoring to compensate, and you may need 3 pie shells instead of 2.

꒞꒰꒞꒰꒞꒰꒞꒰꒞꒰꒞꒰꒞꒰꒞꒰꒞꒰꒞꒰꒞꒰꒞꒰꒞

Wash and peel potatoes and slice them in medium-size chunks. Put in a large boiler and cover with water. Boil over medium heat until tender, until a fork gently inserted in a chunk or two falls through them easily. Drain potatoes and place in large mixing bowl.

Preheat oven to 325 degrees Fahrenheit. Bake pie shells for about 5 minutes, just to firm them up a bit. Use fork to pierce them about 10 or 15 times to minimize buckling and swelling.

Add butter, sugar, cinnamon, nutmeg, and vanilla to the bowl and beat thoroughly. Put eggs in a small bowl and scramble a while, then add them to the pie filling. Use a spoon to stir the eggs into the filling, until it's all completely blended. DO NOT overscramble the eggs, and DO NOT beat them into the filling with the blender.

If your filling isn't sweet enough for you, add 1/4 cup more sugar, then pour into shells and bake for 40 minutes to an hour. They'll puff up slightly in the middle, and perhaps even start to toast a little bit on top when they're done. My goodness, these are good!

Special Potato Salad

When Dr. Kevin starts a quilting group in Green, she is determined that good food will be part of each meeting and wants to make her own special potato salad—which, of course, she has learned from her mother. The recipe below is from Cynthia Ransburg-Brown, a lawyer and mother of two, who, like Kevin, took her mom's recipe and made it her own. Enjoy!

Ingredients:

2 or 3 large baking potatoes (peeled and cut into large chunks)
4 large eggs (boiled and finely chopped)
2 tablespoons of butter or margarine
1 tablespoon sweet pickle relish
1 tablespoon mayonnaise or Miracle Whip
1 tablespoon of sandwich spread
1 teaspoon of yellow mustard
½ teaspoon of Tony's Cajun Seasoning
Salt and pepper to taste

Instructions from Cynthia:

"Cook potatoes in a medium saucepan until a fork can easily pierce the potatoes. Don't cook too long or the salad will become mushy (technical cooking term!). You can also boil the eggs at the same time (even in the same pot). Strain the potatoes using a colander and pour into mixing bowl over the butter. Set aside and allow the butter to melt. In the meantime, you can peel the boiled eggs and chop finely. Mash the potatoes, mixing in the butter while mashing. Add the eggs and remaining ingredients to the bowl and stir like crazy. (I usually sing, 'She works hard for the money!' while doing this part.)

"I usually have to add about one or more teaspoons of relish, mayo, or sandwich spread, but it manages to turn out pretty good each time. I usually garnish lightly with some Tony's or Old Bay Seasoning for color on top. Some people add finely sliced pimentos for color as well.

"This yields a medium-size mixing bowl of salad. I have made it with two potatoes and three eggs, and it fills a small mixing bowl.

"Serve chilled."

Want to learn more about author
Judy Christie and check out other great fiction
from Abingdon Press?

Sign up for our fiction newsletter at
www.AbingdonPress.com
to read interviews with your favorite authors, find tips
for starting a reading group, and stay posted on what
new titles are on the horizon. It's a place to connect
with other fiction readers or post a
comment about this book.

Do you have questions or comments about Green,
Louisiana? Voice them to "Speak Out, Green." Ask
those questions you've always wanted to ask or offer
that opinion you've wanted to voice. E-mail comments to
judy@judychristie.com. Lois, Iris Jo, Tammy, and the
newspaper team say, "Keep it short, keep it sweet, and build
our community up with your comments."
And if you'd like to have author Judy Christie speak to
your book club in person or via conference call, e-mail her at
judy@judychristie.com, too.

Be sure to visit Judy online!

www.judychristie.com

What they're saying about...

Gone to Green, by Judy Christie
"…Refreshingly realistic religious fiction, this novel is unafraid to address the injustices of sexism, racism, and corruption as well as the spiritual devastation that often accompanies the loss of loved ones. Yet these darker narrative tones beautifully highlight the novel's message of friendship, community, and God's reassuring and transformative love." —*Publishers Weekly* **starred review**

The Call of Zulina, by Kay Marshall Strom
"This compelling drama will challenge readers to remember slavery's brutal history, and its heroic characters will inspire them. Highly recommended."
—*Library Journal* **starred review**

Surrender the Wind, by Rita Gerlach
"I am purely a romance reader, and yet you hooked me in with a war scene, of all things! I would have never believed it. You set the mood beautifully and have a clean, strong, lyrical way with words. You have done your research well enough to transport me back to the war-torn period of colonial times."
—Julie Lessman, author of *The Daughters of Boston* series

One Imperfect Christmas, by Myra Johnson
"Debut novelist Myra Johnson ushers us into the Christmas season with a fresh and exciting story that will give you a chuckle and a special warmth."
—DiAnn Mills, author of *Awaken My Heart* and *Breach of Trust*

The Prayers of Agnes Sparrow, by Joyce Magnin
"Beware of *The Prayers of Agnes Sparrow*. Just when you have become fully enchanted by its marvelous quirky zaniness, you will suddenly be taken to your knees by its poignant truth-telling about what it means to be divinely human. I'm convinced that 'on our knees' is exactly where Joyce Magnin planned for us to land all along." —Nancy Rue, co-author of *Healing Waters* (**Sullivan Crisp** Series)
        2009 Novel of the Year

The Fence My Father Built, by Linda S. Clare
"…Linda Clare reminds us with her writing that is wise, funny, and heartbreaking, that what matters most in life are the people we love and the One who gave them to us."—Gina Ochsner, Dark Horse Literary, winner of the Oregon Book Award
        and the Flannery O'Connor Award for Short Fiction

eye of the god, by Ariel Allison
"Filled with action on three continents, *eye of the god* is a riveting fast-paced thriller, but it is Abby—who, in spite of another letdown by a man, remains filled with hope—who makes Ariel Allison's tale a super read."—Harriet Klausner

www.AbingdonPress.com/fiction

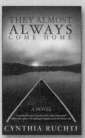